HELP!
I'M TRAPPED IN
OBEDIENCE SCHOOL

Other Books by Todd Strasser

HELP!
I'M TRAPPED IN
OBEDIENCE SCHOOL

TODD STRASSER

AN
APPLE
PAPERBACK

SCHOLASTIC INC.
New York Toronto London Auckland Sydney

ISBN 0-590-97514-5

12 11 10 9 8 7   6 7 8 9/9 0/0

Printed in the U.S.A.   40

First Scholastic printing, September 1995

*To Regina Griffin,
with whom I love to work and laugh.*

"Treat him like a human. Feed him like a dog."
— the Iams Company (Dog Food Manufacturer)

"The more I see of men, the more I admire dogs."
— Madame de Sevigné (Old French Lady)

HELP!
I'M TRAPPED IN
OBEDIENCE SCHOOL

Note

Hi, I'm Jake Sherman. You may have read about me before. I'm the kid who accidentally switched bodies with his dorky science teacher, and then got stuck in the first day of eighth grade.

Well, guess what? It's happened again . . .

1

"**H**as anyone seen my new shoes?" my father asked before dinner one night. He came into the dining room wearing his shirt and tie from work. My sister, Jessica, and I were setting the table for dinner. The scent of roast lamb was in the air.

"Which ones?" Jessica asked. She was in tenth grade and a couple of inches taller than me. She'd gone through a stage where she dyed her hair black and wore earrings in strange parts of her body, but now her hair was brown and she wore it in a thick braid that hung down her back.

"A pair of soft leather loafers," Dad said. "I just bought — " He suddenly stopped talking. His eyes narrowed as he stared down at something.

"Just bought what?" I asked.

"Tell me I'm not seeing this," Dad groaned. He pointed at the low wooden coffee table in the living room. One of the legs looked like a beaver had

3

gnawed on it. Splinters and small hunks of wood lay on the carpet around it.

"Honey?" my father called in that low, solemn voice he only uses when he's super serious.

"Yes?" Mom called from the kitchen.

"You better come in here."

My mother came into the room. Her eyes widened and her jaw dropped. "Oh, no! Not my new coffee table!"

"And I'm missing a brand-new pair of loafers," my father said.

"No, you're not," Jessica said. "You're only missing one loafer."

"What do you mean?" Dad asked.

Jessica pointed to the fireplace. Lying next to it was a mangled brown thing about the size and shape of a shoe. "You just found one."

Clang! From the kitchen came the sound of a metal platter hitting the floor.

"The lamb!" Mom gasped.

We all raced into the kitchen. The platter was upside down on the floor, and the tiles were covered with gravy. In the middle of it all, Lance was gnawing on the roast lamb. Lance was our one-year-old yellow Labrador retriever. He weighed seventy-five pounds and had a coat of short fur. When he wasn't chewing on dinner, shoes, or table legs, he was a pretty good pet.

"That's it." My father crossed his arms firmly. "This dog is gone."

4

Jessica and I looked at each other in horror.

"Where?" my sister gasped.

"To my brother's farm," Dad said. "Don't say I didn't warn you."

It was true. The week before, Lance had chewed up a brand-new baseball mitt, a pair of hiking boots, and the handle of my father's favorite umbrella. Dad had warned us that if we didn't get him to stop wrecking stuff, we might have to get rid of him.

"Oh, Dad, please don't." Jessica started to cry.

Of course, that always softened Dad up. "Well, you have to do *something* about this dog."

"Perhaps it's time to consider obedience school," Mom said.

2

"**O**bedience school?" my friend Josh Hopka said the next day in science lab. Josh was a little on the chubby side, with reddish hair and freckles. I had just told him what happened the night before. "What good is that going to do?"

"It'll teach him to be obedient," I said as I peered into a microscope.

"Has anyone found an amoeba?" our teacher, Mr. Dirksen, asked. He was walking around the lab wearing a white coat.

"Yes!" Julia Saks raised her hand and pointed at Alex Silver. "He's right there."

The class cracked up.

"Get stuffed, Julia," Alex muttered.

"Let's be serious, class," Mr. Dirksen said, but that was a joke. Mr. Dirksen never got any respect. He used to be bald and wear thick glasses. Then he and I accidentally switched bodies when lightning hit the experiment he was doing at home. It was really weird to be Mr. Dirksen for a few days, and after we switched back I had a much better understanding of what it was like to be a grown-up nerd. So did Mr. Dirksen, which was why he now wore contacts and a rug on his head.

But even with the toupee and no glasses, Mr. Dirksen still got more grief than any other teacher at Burt Itchupt Middle School.

"You think obedience school will stop Lance from chewing on stuff?" Josh whispered.

"Why not?" asked Andy Kent, who was my other best friend. Andy was taller than me, with black hair and braces.

"Because it's in a dog's genes to chew," Josh said. "It's the way they're programmed. They *have* to chew."

"When did *you* become such an expert?" I asked.

"Please stop talking, boys," Mr. Dirksen said.

"I think I found one!" Amber Sweeney called out.

Mr. Dirksen went over and pressed his eye against Amber's microscope. "Where?"

"See that big blob?" Amber asked.

Mr. Dirksen's forehead wrinkled. "That's a blob, all right, but it's a blob of nothing."

"A big blob o' nothin'," Andy said with a yawn. He put his hand over his mouth.

"Up late last night?" I asked.

"Yeah," he said. "Now move over, it's my turn."

I backed away from the microscope and let Andy have a look.

"You think obedience school is going to teach Lance not to eat roast lamb?" Josh asked. "If you had a choice between lamb and that dog food junk you feed him, which would *you* choose?"

"I'm not a dog," I said.

"That's a subject for debate," Andy whispered, scratching his head. His hair looked sort of greasy, like he hadn't washed it in a long time.

"Andy, Josh, and Jake — I said enough talking," Mr. Dirksen warned. I stopped talking. Ever since he and I switched bodies, I tried not to give him a hard time. After all, I'd been a teacher for a few days. It wasn't easy.

"This is dumb, Mr. Dork . . . er, Dirksen," Josh said. "What are Jake and I supposed to do while Andy looks in the microscope?"

"Help him," Mr. Dirksen said.

"Hey! I think I see something!" Andy cried.

"What?" Josh and I crowded around him.

"Aw, nuts." Andy sounded disappointed. "It's just a big blob o' nothin'."

"The Dorkhead's a big blob o' nothin'," Josh grumbled.

"Leave him alone," I said. "He's just trying to do his job. You think it's easy to teach a bunch of geeks like us?"

"Oh, wow!" Andy gasped.

"Now what?" Josh asked.

"That big blob o' nothin' just became a big blob o' somethin'! And not only that, it's growing a baby blob!"

"Lemme see!" Josh pushed him out of the way, peered down into the microscope, then waved at our teacher. "Hey, Mr. Dork . . . I mean, Mr. Dirksen! We got a baby blob growing over here!"

"That would be highly unusual," Mr. Dirksen said as he came toward us. "Amoebas are neither male nor female. They don't have babies. Instead they divide by fission into new cells of equal size."

"Oh yeah? Then what's that?" Josh pointed into the microscope's eyepiece.

Mr. Dirksen squinted down into the microscope. "Ah! *That* is a pseudopod!"

"A pseudopod?" Josh gasped.

"A big blob o' pseudo!" Andy cried, sticking his finger in the air.

"The pseudo of pod!" yelled Josh. The school theater had just performed *The Wizard of Oz*, and the songs were still fresh in our minds. Josh and Andy hooked arms and started to sing:

> *We're off to see the pseudo*
> *The wonderful pseudo of pod*
> *We hear he is a wonderful pod*
> *If ever a pseudo there was.*
> *If ever oh-ever a pseudo there was,*
> *The pseudo of pod is one because*

> *Because, because, because, because,*
> *because . . .*
> *Because of the wonderful things he*
> *does!*

"Stop it!" Mr. Dirksen ordered.

But it was too late. Now the whole class joined in, dancing and singing around the lab.

> *We're off to see the pseudo*
> *The wonderful pseudo of pod . . .*

"I said, stop it!" Mr. Dirksen shouted. I felt bad for him, but there was nothing I could do.

Meanwhile, Mr. Dirksen's face turned red. "If you don't stop it right now, I'll — "

Flap! On the other side of the room, one of the shades suddenly shot up. It spun around, then broke off its mounts, bounced off the radiator, and smashed into the window, shattering the glass.

"Yeah!" "All right!" "Ya-hoo!" The class broke into loud cheers. Mr. Dirksen went over to his desk and buried his head in his hands.

"I give up!" he groaned.

3

"**G**imme the ball! Gimme the ball!" Josh yelled.

Groof! Groof! Groof! Behind the backyard fence Lance barked at us.

In our driveway, Alex faked left and passed the basketball to Josh.

Groof! Groof! Groof! Lance put his front paws on the fence and barked like crazy.

Josh pivoted to shoot, but Andy was all over him.

"You'll never sink it," Andy needled him. "You'll bite the big crusty. You'll miss by a mile."

Groof! Groof! Groof! Lance barked.

"Here! Pass it back!" Alex cut past me and waved his arms.

Groof! Groof! Groof!

Josh twisted to his right, then to his left, but Andy stayed right on him.

"You rot, Josh. You couldn't sink a rock in the ocean."

"Here! Pass it!" Alex backed around me.

Groof! Groof! Groof!

"Your mother has a better shot than you!"

"Here! Here! I'm wide open!"

Groof! Groof! Groof!

Instead of passing the ball to Alex, Josh twisted awkwardly and tried an impossible one-handed, off-balance, fadeaway jumper.

"Airball!" Andy yelled. The ball missed the rim. He caught it and put in an easy layup.

"All right!" he cheered. The game was over. For the first time in weeks, he and I had defeated Josh and Alex.

"The new intergalactic champions of Jeffersonville, the United States, the world, *and* the universe!" Andy shouted as he and I exchanged double high fives.

Josh glowered at Alex. "Way to go, jerkface."

"What!?" Alex looked shocked that Josh had blamed *him* for the loss. "I was wide open. All you had to do was pass it."

"You weren't open for a second," Josh said.

"Was too!" Alex said. "I had Jake totally fooled."

Andy and I stopped celebrating. Everything around us grew quiet. Even Lance stopped barking.

"You always have to showboat," Alex said. "You always have to put in the winning shot, Mr. Cool. And if something goes wrong, it's always someone else's fault."

Josh glared at him. "Drop dead, Alex." He stomped away down the driveway.

"Here we go again." Andy sighed.

"Just admit it for once, Josh," Alex yelled after him. "You choked. It's no one else's fault."

Halfway down the driveway, Josh wheeled around. His face was red. "No way. Maybe I just can't take all the noise. Andy and his nonstop trash talk. You yelling for the ball every second, and that stupid dog barking all the time."

"Now it's the dog's fault," Andy quipped.

"Hey, it's a lot worse in the pros," I said.

"We're not in the pros, okay?" Josh snapped at me. "We're just some eighth-graders trying to play a little two-on-two in a driveway."

Alex looked at his watch. "Well, this eighth-grader has to bag it. See you at school tomorrow." He picked up his shirt and went down the driveway.

"Wuss," Josh muttered as Alex passed him.

"Bonehead," Alex growled back.

"Barfbreath."

"Dorkbrain."

"Pseudopod."

"Nematode."

Andy and I gave each other a look. It seemed like some things would never change.

4

We took a break and got a drink from the hose next to the garage. Behind the fence, Lance lapped up some water from his bowl and then stretched out in the sun for a nap.

"Man, what a life." Andy wiped the sweat off his forehead and nodded at Lance. "He gets to play all day, and sleep whenever he wants. Wish I could do that."

"You come pretty close," Josh said, then turned to me. "Every night his head hits the pillow and he's out like a light. He doesn't even wash."

"Hey, I wash when I need to," Andy said.

"When's that?" Josh asked. "Every New Year's Eve? Look at those fingernails. Is that the grossest thing you ever saw? Don't you ever cut them?"

Andy used to bite his nails. But then he stopped. Now they were long and had black crescents of dirt under them.

"It's better this way than biting them," Andy said.

14

"You see that shirt?" Josh pointed at Andy's white *No Fear* T-shirt. "This is the third day in a row he's worn it."

"So?" Andy said. "It doesn't smell."

"Not to you," said Josh.

"What's your problem, Josh?" Andy asked. "How come you always have to put everyone else down?"

I figured it was time to change the subject before those two got into a fight.

"So when are your parents coming home?" I asked Andy. His parents had taken his little brother out of school and gone to visit relatives. Andy couldn't miss school, so he was staying at Josh's house until they came back.

"Two nights from tonight." Andy pulled a pack of Skittles from his pocket and tore it open. "Want some?"

Josh and I held out our hands and Andy poured a few into our palms.

"I bet you guys are having a blast." I popped some of the candies into my mouth. Josh's parents worked late every night. So Josh and Andy had the house to themselves.

"It's okay," Josh said. "But with school every day and homework every night we can't do that much."

"Yeah, even when there are no parents around, you still have responsibilities." Andy pointed at Lance, stretched out in the sun, asleep. "It's not like being a dog. Then you can lie around all day and sleep and eat and play — "

"And never take a bath," Josh added.

"Drop dead, Josh." Andy smirked. "And the best part is you never have to go to school. *That's* the life."

I picked up the basketball and tossed it to him. "How about playing Horse?"

"Okay." Andy shot the ball at the basket.

Groof! Groof! Groof! As soon as the ball left Andy's hands, Lance woke up and started barking and wagging his tail. His mouth was open and his tongue hung out. *Groof! Groof! Groof!*

Josh shook his head in disgust. "What's with that dumb dog?"

"He just wants to play," Andy said.

Groof! Groof! Groof! Somehow Lance always knew when we were talking about him. He wagged his tail faster and eagerly scratched the gate with his paw.

"What a pain," Josh groaned.

"No, he's not," said my sister Jessica as she came out the kitchen door.

Groof! Groof! Groof! Lance barked at her. Jessica kneeled down next to him, put her arm around his neck, and gave him a hug.

"Boy, I wish she'd do that to me," Andy mumbled out of the corner of his mouth.

"Hey, watch it," I warned him. I didn't like my friends making cracks about my big sister.

"He's my love puppy," Jessica cooed, kissing Lance on the head. "My big, big poochy poo." She rubbed his head. "Right, Lancey Wancey?"

"Lancey Wancey?" Josh whispered and made a face.

"It's a girl thing." I shrugged.

Lance rolled onto his back so that Jessica could scratch his tummy.

"Hey, Jessica," Andy said. "We're trying to play a little B-ball but Lance keeps barking so much, it's impossible."

"He hasn't gotten out today," Jessica replied. "Maybe if Jake took him to the park and let him run around he wouldn't bark so much."

"Why don't *you* take him?" I said.

"Because I walk him all the time and you never do," Jessica answered. "Besides, Mom called and said she and Dad are coming home late tonight. I have to make dinner."

It seemed only fair that if she was going to cook, I should walk the dog. I turned to Josh and Andy. "What do you think?"

"Might as well," Josh said. "We can't play basketball with all that racket."

5

Jessica got the leash and tossed it to me. "Have fun."

"Right," I muttered and opened the gate.

Lance shot out of the gate and headed straight for Josh.

"Hey, get down, you dumb mutt!" Josh shouted as Lance jumped up on him and tried to lick his face. Lance backed down to all fours but he was still smiling and wagging his tail excitedly.

"Why does he always jump up on me?" Josh asked, wiping the dirty paw marks off his white T-shirt.

"Maybe he's in love," Andy said with a grin.

"And maybe you're a geek," Josh shot back.

I clipped the leash to Lance's collar and we started walking toward the park. Well, actually, Lance pretty much *dragged* me. He pulled so hard that it took all my strength to stop him from yanking the leash out of my hand.

"Why does he keep pulling so hard?" Josh

asked. "Doesn't he understand that you've got the leash?"

"He's only one year old," I tried to explain. "He doesn't know any better — *whoa!*"

Lance jerked the leash out of my hand and took off after a squirrel, who quickly scampered up a tree.

Groof! Groof! Groof! Lance stood on his hind legs and pressed his front paws against the tree trunk, barking up at the squirrel.

"Hey, Lance!" I called and clapped my hands. "Come on back, Lance. Here boy!"

Groof! Groof! Groof! Lance kept barking up the tree.

"Come on, Lance, over here!" I yelled.

"You really expect him to come?" Josh asked doubtfully.

"We figure if we keep calling him, maybe he'll understand someday," I said.

"Yeah, right." Josh rolled his eyes like he didn't believe it.

"He can learn stuff." I walked over to the tree, picked up the leash, and pulled Lance back toward Josh and Andy. "Watch this. Okay, Lance, sit."

Lance stood and wagged his tail with that big dumb smile on his face.

"Sit! Come on, *sit!*" I yelled.

Lance sat and panted with his tongue hanging out.

"See?" I said. "He listens." No sooner were the

words out of my mouth than Lance dashed off after another squirrel.

"Oh, yeah, he listens." Josh smirked.

"Why do you always have to be so negative?" Andy asked him.

"Because Jake lives in a dream world," Josh said.

"Why, just because he proved that Lance listens?"

"He didn't prove squat."

"Would you guys both chill?" I asked.

Josh and Andy glared at each other.

"Dimwit," Josh mumbled.

"Dweeb," Andy muttered back.

"Scuzzball."

"Fungus."

"Jerk."

"Geek."

Meanwhile, I found an old tennis ball lying near a tree. "Maybe he'll fetch. Hey, Lance! Fetch!"

I threw the ball. Lance took off and got it.

"Okay, boy!" I shouted. "Bring it back!"

Lance trotted back to us and stopped about ten feet away.

"Good boy. Now give me the ball." I stepped toward him, but Lance immediately backed away with his tail wagging and the ball clenched tightly in his teeth. Then he put the ball on the ground and crouched down behind it, watching me carefully.

"Come on, give me the ball." I stepped closer, but every time I got near Lance, he would grab the ball in his teeth and jump away, wagging his tail playfully.

"He thinks you want to play keep away." Josh shook his head. "I'm telling you, Jake. This is one hopeless mutt."

6

We played around in the park for a while, chasing Lance and getting him to chase us.

"So when does Lance start obedience school?" Andy asked.

"Tonight," I said. "Turns out they've just started a course over at the church. The first class was last week, but they said we could start a week late."

"Dorksen probably wishes he could send us there, too," Josh said.

"You really ought to give the guy a break," I said. "He's just trying to do his job."

"What's with you, Jake?" Andy asked. "Since when do you go around defending teachers? Especially meganerds like Dorksen?"

"Yeah, he's the worst pseudopod of all," said Josh.

"Just a big blob o' pseudopod," added Andy. Even though he and Josh had just argued, now they grinned and gave each other high fives.

Andy and Josh were my best friends, but I'd never told them about the time Mr. Dirksen and I switched bodies. I'd come close to telling them many times, but I'd always stopped myself, knowing that they'd never believe me.

"I'm just saying it's not easy to be a teacher," I said. "Think about it. Every year you have to deal with a new bunch of phlegmwads like us who don't want to be in school. It must be a real drag."

"If it's so bad, why doesn't he get a different job?" Andy asked.

"Because he's dedicated," I said. "Because he thinks it's important that we get educated."

Josh studied me for a second. "How do *you* know what Dorksen thinks?"

"Because I do," I said.

Andy and Josh gave each other funny looks.

"Listen, Jake," Josh said. "We're your friends, okay? We're not going to grade you. You don't have to be the teacher's pet with us."

"I'm not being the teacher's pet," I said. "It's the truth. You've never been in Mr. Dirksen's shoes. I'm pretty sure you'd feel a lot different if you knew what it was like on his side of the desk."

Josh nudged Andy. "Listen to him. The voice of authority."

"Yeah," said Andy. "It's not like *you've* been in his shoes either, Jake."

I couldn't help what I said next. "Actually, I have."

7

"Let me make sure I've got this right," Josh said a little while later as we walked toward Mr. Dirksen's house. "You're saying you and Dorksen actually switched bodies?"

"Yup." I was standing near a fire hydrant, which Lance had stopped to sniff.

"I hate to say this, Jake," Andy said. "But I think you've gone mental."

"You'll see," I said, tugging on the leash to get Lance away from the hydrant.

"This is stupid," Josh complained. "You don't really expect us to believe this, do you?"

"You'll see," I said.

"You'll see, you'll see," Josh mimicked me.

"Seriously, Jake," Andy said. "Let's get real for a second. This isn't *The X-Files*. In real life people don't switch bodies."

"That's what I thought, too," I said.

Andy and Josh gave each other doubtful looks.

Up ahead was Mr. Dirksen's small brown house. I turned up the driveway with Lance.

Josh stopped behind me. "You can't just go into his house."

"It's in the garage," I said. "Besides, now that Mr. Dirksen is married to Ms. Rogers, he doesn't spend much time here."

Josh and Andy hesitated.

"You guys chicken?" I asked.

"This is trespassing," Josh said.

"No, it's not," I said. "Dirksen knows us. Besides, we're not going to do anything wrong. I'm just going to show you the experiment."

Josh and Andy started up Mr. Dirksen's driveway while I lifted the garage door. The experiment took up most of the garage. It consisted of two metal cages with tons of wires and computer consoles in between.

"Whoa!" Josh gasped. "What is this?"

"I told you," I said. "This is how Mr. Dirksen and I switched bodies."

Josh rolled his eyes in disbelief. "Yeah, right."

"Hey, chill." Andy smiled and winked at him. Then he turned to me. "So tell us the story, Jake."

"Well, remember the day we shot the spitballs at the blackboard and I hit Dirksen by accident?" I said. "You guys got away, but I got caught. My punishment was to carry a magnetic resonance oscilloscope here because Dirksen's back hurt and he couldn't carry it. Then he asked me to stay and help him. I was working on one cage. He was working on the other."

"So, you were over here," Andy said with a big smile as he walked over to the cage nearest him. Then he pointed at the other cage, where Lance was sniffing around. "And Dorksen was over there?"

"Right."

"I know," Josh said with a grin as he stepped over to a large red electrical switch. "It was like *Frankenstein*. You guys were at the cages and the hunchback threw the switch."

I'd never seen that switch before. It must have been new. I didn't know what it was for. "I wouldn't — "

Too late. Josh pulled the switch down.

Whhhuuuummmpppp!

A huge jolt knocked me to the floor. For a second, everything went black.

8

When I opened my eyes the garage was filled with a strange-smelling haze. It wasn't like smoke, but more like a thick mist. It smelled like air after a thunderstorm. Josh was sitting on the floor near me with a surprised look on his face. I quickly turned and looked at Andy. He had been knocked to the floor, too, and had a startled look on *his* face.

"What happened?" Josh asked.

Before I could answer, Andy got to his hands and feet and scrambled across the garage on all fours. He ran like a bear or something.

"What's with him?" Josh got to his feet and brushed himself off.

"Guess he just got freaked," I said as Andy continued down the driveway on his hands and feet. "Throwing that switch was a real stroke of genius, Josh."

"Hey, I didn't think anything would happen,"

Josh said. But he looked a little worried. "You should have warned me."

"Warn you?" I asked. "How was I supposed to know you were going to pull it? I didn't even know what it was. I never saw it before."

Screech! Honk! At the end of the driveway, a car screeched to a halt and narrowly missed hitting Andy, who was crossing the street on his hands and feet.

"What's with that kid?" Josh asked, shaking his head.

I started to answer, but just then something tapped me on the shoulder. I turned around. Lance was standing behind me.

And I mean, standing!

9

" **A** *h!*" I let out a yell of surprise and jumped back. On his hind feet, Lance was almost as tall as Josh.

"Why's he standing like that?" Josh asked nervously.

Yip . . . raar . . . grurf . . . furf . . . Lance was making weird noises. *Grurf . . . arfff . . . fruff . . .*

"Sounds like he's trying to talk," Josh said.

Whatever Lance was trying to do, he wasn't making much sense. The weird thing was, he seemed to *know* that he wasn't making much sense. Still standing on his hind legs, he pointed out of the garage with one of his forepaws.

I looked in the direction Lance was pointing. Andy was sitting on the lawn across the street. He stuck his nose in the air as if he was sniffing something.

Then he lifted his left leg and bent his head

toward it. His foot bicycled as if he was trying to scratch his ear.

Like a dog or something . . .

I looked back at Lance, who was standing with his paws on his hips.

Like a person or something . . .

10

"Oh, no!" I started to feel faint.

"What's wrong?" Josh asked.

"Don't you know what happened?"

"I, uh, I flicked the switch," Josh said. "But it was *your* fault."

"Josh, shut up and look at Lance."

Lance, my dog, was still standing on his hind feet. Only now he'd crossed his arms.

"Now look at Andy," I said.

On the lawn across the street, Andy was lying on his stomach, but propped up on his elbows like a sphinx. His mouth was open and his tongue was hanging out.

Josh blinked. "No way! This is a joke, right? Like you and Andy got together and planned this, right?"

Lance walked over and tapped Josh on the shoulder as if to say, "What about me?"

"*Ah!*" Josh spun around and jumped away. "Hey, Jake, tell him to back off!"

"Stop it," I said to Lance. "You're freaking out Josh."

Lance shrugged and raised his paws in a helpless gesture. Josh watched him, wide-eyed. "How'd he learn to do that? How'd he learn to stand on his hind legs and act like a human?"

"Guess," I said.

"No." Josh shook his head. "Forget it. Not possible. This is a joke. It's a good one, Jake. Nice going, now let's chill, okay?"

Groof! Groof! barked Lance.

Josh gave me a nervous look. "What'd he say?"

"I don't know for sure, but I have a feeling it was, 'This is no joke.' "

Lance nodded.

"No, this can't be happening!" Josh groaned.

Groof! Lance pointed with his paw across the street. Andy was now lying on his side on the lawn. His legs and arms stuck out at right angles to his body and his eyes were closed.

Josh looked back at Lance and me. "But it's still a joke, right? That's why I'm the only one who's totally freaked by this, right?"

"Believe me, I'm freaked, too," I said. "It's just that I've seen it before. And Andy's not freaked because he's not Andy. He's Lance, and Lance probably doesn't have a clue about what's going on."

"Okay," Josh said, "but if Andy is now in Lance's body, how come he's not freaking out?"

We both turned and looked at Lance, who was still standing with his arms crossed.

Groof! barked Lance, I mean, Andy, I mean, Lance.

"What'd he say?" Josh asked.

"How should I know?" I said. "I can't talk to dogs."

"Take a guess."

"Okay, maybe he said he isn't freaked," I said.

Groof! Lance shook his head.

"Okay, maybe you are freaked," I said.

Arf! Lance nodded.

"He's not *acting* freaked," Josh said.

"How's he *supposed* to act?" I asked.

"I don't know. Maybe he's supposed to run around and chase his tail or something. I mean, if I were in his shoes I'd be totally *mega*-freaked."

I gave Lance a questioning look.

Groof! Lance shook his head.

"Maybe he isn't totally mega-freaked because he knows all we have to do is get him and Andy, I mean, Lance, back into the experiment and switch their bodies back," I guessed.

Arf! Arf! Lance nodded and barked eagerly.

"Okay, then let's do it," Josh said. "I promised his parents nothing bad would happen while he stayed with us. If they come back and find out he's a dog, I think they might be just *a little* upset."

33

11

Josh, Lance, and I started down Mr. Dirksen's driveway. Suddenly Josh stopped and turned to Lance. "Could you do me a favor?"

Groof? Lance barked.

"Could you walk like a normal dog?" Josh asked. "It's really annoying when you walk on two feet."

"It might be a good idea," I agreed. "Just in case someone sees you."

Lance let out a big sigh, as if he was trying to decide what to do. You could see he wasn't happy about walking like a dog.

"Look, Andy," Josh said. "If you're going to be a dog, you might as well act like one."

Groof! Lance barked back, a little indignantly, I thought.

"What'd he say?" asked Josh.

"I think he said, 'Mind your own business.' "

Arf! Lance nodded.

We crossed the street to the lawn where Andy was lying with his eyes closed and a big smile on his face. Every few moments his legs or arms would twitch.

"Looks like he's dreaming," I said.

"You think he's dreaming about human stuff or dog stuff?" Josh asked.

"Well, since he's now a dog in a human body, I'd guess dog stuff."

"We better wake him." Josh nudged Andy's shoulder with his foot. "Get up, dude."

Andy opened his eyes. He turned his head and looked up at us. He opened his mouth, let his tongue hang out and started to pant. Then he stretched his legs and got up.

Ruff! He jumped up and put his hands on Josh's shoulders, knocking him backwards.

"Cut it out!" Josh yelled.

Andy got down on his hands and feet again. He started to shake his rear end back and forth.

"Now what's he doing?" Josh asked.

"I guess he's wagging his tail," I said.

"He doesn't *have* a tail!"

"Tell him that."

"This is the stupidest thing I ever saw," Josh groaned.

Ruff! Ruff! Andy barked playfully.

"Why doesn't he talk?" Josh asked.

"He doesn't know he can."

Josh shook his head in disgust. "For a dog in a human body, you are really dumb."

"He doesn't understand a word you're saying,"

I said. "Let's just get him into the garage and switch him back into Andy."

I stepped toward Andy, but he quickly jumped away, wiggling his rear back and forth.

Ruff! Ruff! he barked.

"Uh-oh. He wants to play," I said.

Groof! Groof! Lance barked angrily.

"What'd he say?" Josh asked.

"My guess is it was something like, 'Stop fooling around, you dumb dog, this is serious.' "

Arf! Lance nodded.

"Okay, let's get him!" Josh lunged at Andy and tried to tackle him, but Andy darted away. I tried to grab him too, but he slipped through my grip.

Ruff! Ruff! Still on all fours, still shaking his rear end, Andy barked happily at us. He obviously thought this was a great game.

"This is ridiculous," Josh insisted. "It's two guys and a dog against one guy. We should be able to get him."

Groof! Lance shook his head.

"Now what?" Josh asked.

"I think he feels it's *three* guys against one *dog*," I said.

"Look," Josh said. "It doesn't matter what it is. The only thing that matters is getting him into the garage and switching him back."

"Okay, spread out," I said. "We'll surround him."

Josh, Lance, and I spread out around Andy,

who just smiled and panted and shook his rear like this was terrific fun.

"Okay, guys," I said. "On the count of three, we all rush him. One, two — "

"Jake!" a voice called out. "Hey, Jake!"

I turned around and looked down the street. Someone was coming toward us. It was Jessica!

12

"**W**hat do we do?" Josh gasped.

I quickly turned to Lance, who was still standing on his hind legs. "Act like a dog," I whispered.

Groof! Lance shook his head.

"I mean it," I hissed. "If you don't start acting like a dog, you may never get back into your old body."

Lance looked pretty peeved, but at least he got down on all fours. Meanwhile, Jessica walked quickly toward us.

"I've been looking all over for you," she said. "You didn't forget about obedience school, did you?"

"Uh . . . of course not," I said. The truth was I'd totally forgotten about it.

"Well, it starts in ten minutes." My sister bent down and picked up Lance's leash. "We better — "

She stopped talking and stared at Andy, who

was walking toward her on his hands and feet, shaking his rear. His mouth was open, his tongue was hanging out, and he was panting happily.

"What's his problem?" Jessica asked.

"Well, you see . . . er . . ." Not knowing what to say, I gave Josh a panicked look.

"Uh . . . it's for the school play," Josh said.

"Oh, yeah," I said. "Andy's practicing his part."

"He's a dog in the school play?" Jessica frowned. Meanwhile, Andy started to sniff her leg. "What play?"

Josh and I looked at each other in horror. We didn't know any plays.

"Uh . . . *Of Mice and Men*," Josh said.

"Huh?" Jessica looked at him like he was crazy. "There's no dog in that play."

"Oh . . . uh . . . well, er, you see, they didn't have anyone who could play the mouse," Josh said.

"Yeah, that's right," I said. "So they decided to change the mouse to a dog."

"Andy's really good at playing dogs," Josh added.

Andy was kneeling at Jessica's feet, sniffing her shoes.

"I get the picture, Andy," Jessica said. "You can stop now."

Of course, Andy didn't stop. He kept right on sniffing.

"Come on, Andy, you heard her." Josh reached

down, grabbed the collar of Andy's shirt and yanked him up. Andy straightened up and stood on his feet. But his mouth was still open and his tongue was still hanging out.

Ruff! he barked happily.

Jessica kept staring at him.

"Uh, when Andy has a part in a play, he really gets into the role," I said.

Ruff! Andy barked again. He tried to step toward Jessica, but Josh held him firmly by the collar and yanked him back.

"I think it's time for me and Andy to go home," Josh said. Still holding Andy by the collar, he turned around and started down the sidewalk. Andy looked back over his shoulder at us with that dumb open-mouthed grin on his face.

Ruff! he barked.

I grinned sheepishly at Jessica. "Crazy guy, huh?"

My sister didn't smile. "You're all dementos."

I had a feeling it was time to change the subject. "So, uh, guess we better get over to the church, huh?"

Jessica nodded and tugged on the leash. "Come on, Lance."

But Lance sat down on the lawn and wouldn't budge.

13

"Come on, Lance." Jessica tugged on the leash. Lance pulled back and shook his head.

My sister turned to me. "Now what?"

"Maybe he doesn't want to go to obedience school," I said.

Jessica rolled her eyes. "He's a dog, Jake. He doesn't even know what obedience school is." She tugged on the leash again. "Now come on, Lance, we're going."

Lance dug his nails into the lawn and resisted.

"I don't believe this," my sister groaned.

"Maybe he just doesn't need obedience school anymore," I said.

"I have news for you, Jake. Last night Dad said that Lance was going to obedience school. If he doesn't, he's going to end up on Uncle Jack's farm."

I turned to Lance. "Hear that?"

Groof! Lance barked back stubbornly.

"He does too have a farm!" I said.

Groof! Groof!

"Oh, yeah? Well, you *better* believe it," I warned him.

"Ahem." Jessica cleared her throat. "Is it my imagination, Jake, or are you arguing with a dog?"

"Uh . . . er . . . sometimes I think he understands a lot more than we think he does."

"Oh, sure." Jessica smirked. "Next thing I know you'll be telling me he's in a play, also."

"Hey, you never know," I said.

"Know what I know?" my sister asked. "You and your friends are really losing it. Now we better get to the church before we're late."

Once again, Jessica tugged on the leash, but Lance still wouldn't budge.

"What is with you?" my sister asked Lance irately.

I could see that this was going to be a problem. "Uh, could you leave us alone for a second?"

"You and Lance?" Jessica scowled.

"Yeah, I, uh, think I can make him understand, but it has to be in private."

My sister looked at me like I was nuts. "Are you feeling okay?"

"Just leave us alone."

"Right." Jessica nodded in disbelief. "Anything you say, Mr. Demento." She backed away down the sidewalk.

As soon as she was out of earshot, I kneeled down and got face-to-face with Lance. "Now listen up, dogface," I whispered. "You better come to obedience school, understand?"

Groof! Lance shook his head.

"I don't care whether you think you need it or not," I said. "If you don't go, Dad's going to send you to his brother's farm. You'll probably wind up living in a doghouse with a bunch of mangy old mutts, fighting over food and getting fleas. And forget about ever getting back into your own body again."

Groof! Groof! Lance barked angrily.

"Of course we're going to get you back into your own body," I whispered. "But we're going to have to wait until the time's right. In the meantime, all you have to do is act like a dog. Now come on."

I pulled on the leash, but Lance still wouldn't move.

"You're acting like a real jerk, know that?" I said crossly.

Instead of barking, Lance scratched at his collar with his rear paw.

"Hey, forget it," I said. "You have to wear that collar. It's got your license on it. It's like, the law, dude."

Groof! Lance barked and scratched again at the snap that connected the leash to the collar.

"It's the leash you don't want?"

Arf! Lance nodded.

"Okay, I'll take it off, but only if you promise not to run away."

Lance looked at me like I was an idiot.

"Hey!" I snapped irritably as I took off the leash. "I'm really getting tired of those looks from everyone. Now cut it out!"

Lance shrugged and walked alongside me toward Jessica.

"You took his leash off?" she asked, surprised.

"Yeah, we had a talk. I don't think he'll run away."

Jessica stared at me like I was from another planet. "Sure, Jake."

We got to the church and walked around to the rear entrance near the parking lot. Just ahead of us, a woman with blond hair got out of a car with a gray and white husky.

Woof! Woof! Woof! As soon as the husky saw Lance, he barked and lunged toward him.

"Stop it, Freddy!" the woman yelled and yanked hard on his leash. Meanwhile, Lance hid behind me with his tail between his legs.

"Sorry," the woman apologized. "Freddy's just young and frisky. I guess that's why we're all here, huh?"

"I guess," I said.

Woof! Woof! Freddy must have smelled the other dogs because he started to wag his tail and pull on the leash, dragging the blond woman toward the rear door of the church. The woman looked back at us and scowled, probably because

Lance seemed so well-behaved compared to her dog. Even Jessica looked down at Lance with a puzzled expression on her face.

"Why isn't Lance getting excited?" she asked.

"Did *you* ever get excited about going to school?" I asked.

We went through the door and into the church basement. All the tables and chairs had been pushed to one end of the room, leaving the floor open. Leaning against one wall were some yellow and blue hula hoops. On the floor, a large square had been marked off with orange plastic cones.

About ten other dogs of every imaginable size were already there. Their owners were standing along the walls, holding their leashes tightly. The dogs were yapping and barking and pulling at their leashes as they tried to sniff each other. Their owners were yelling at them to "sit" and "stay."

Jessica and I found a spot along the wall. Lance sat down without being asked and glanced around nervously. Jessica gave him another funny look.

A thin lady wearing jeans and a T-shirt with a silhouette of a poodle on it came up to us. She had wiry white hair that sort of looked like poodle hair to me. In one hand she carried some shiny steel chain collars.

"Hi, I'm Joan Pudlhafer. You must be Jessica Sherman," she said. Then she looked down at Lance. "And this must be your Lab, Lance."

Lance sat there with an apprehensive look on his face.

The lines in Ms. Poodlehair's forehead deepened. "How old did you say he was?"

"About a year," Jessica said.

"Not very frisky for a one-year-old, is he?"

"Well, usually he is," Jessica said.

"You don't think he's sick or anything?" Ms. Poodlehair asked, kneeling down for a closer look.

"No, he's just not himself today," I said. "But I think he'll be okay."

"All right." Ms. Poodlehair stood up and handed Jessica one of the chain collars. It had a chrome ring on either end. "This is a choke collar. Every dog who takes the course gets one free. You put it around Lance's neck and clip the leash to it."

"Why?" I asked.

"This is how we train the dogs to follow commands," she explained. "When you want Lance to obey you, you just give the leash a good yank."

"But won't that choke him?" Jessica asked.

"The dogs feel some tightening around the neck, but we'd never do anything to harm them."

Lance backed behind my legs and whimpered.

"Does he *have* to wear it?" I asked.

"If he didn't need it, he wouldn't need this class," Ms. Poodlehair replied and moved on to the next dog owner.

"Here you go, Lance." Jessica bent down and

tried to put the chain collar around his neck, but Lance turned his head away and wouldn't let her.

"Let me try." I took the choke collar from Jessica and kneeled down in front of Lance. He gave me a really sad look. I knew how he must have felt. After all, I'd once been stuck in Mr. Dirksen's body. If Andy in Lance's body could have talked, I bet he would have said, "Help! I'm trapped in obedience school!"

I held the choke collar up, and Lance gave me another woeful look.

"Just fake it, okay?" I whispered.

Lance shook his head.

"You *have* to."

Groof!

He was really starting to tick me off. "Look, pretend this is regular school, okay? Every day you have to bring your books, right? You have to go to your classes, and do your homework."

Groof!

"Well, you're *supposed* to do your homework," I said. "I mean, those are the rules. This is a school, too. And they have rules here."

"Uh, Jake?" Jessica whispered.

"Just a second," I said and turned back to Lance. "Now, I'm really getting tired of your attitude. If you want us to do what *you* want, then maybe you ought to try doing what *we* want, too."

"Uh, Jake . . ." Jessica spoke more loudly.

"I said, just a second."

"I don't think so," Jessica hissed.

"What?" I looked up at her.

"Look around."

I turned around. The whole room had gone quiet. Even the dogs had become still. Everyone was staring at . . . me!

14

"**O**h, uh, sorry, everyone." I felt my face turn red as I straightened up.

"Do you always talk to him like he's a human?" Ms. Poodlehair asked.

"Not always," I said. "Only when he's not behaving."

Some of the other dog owners smiled.

"He's still not wearing his collar," Ms. Poodlehair reminded me.

I looked down at Lance and narrowed my eyes so he'd know I was totally serious. Lance sighed and nodded. I slipped the choke collar around his neck and clipped it to the leash.

Ms. Poodlehair went to the middle of the room. "Okay, everyone, let's review what we learned last week. Order your dog to sit."

Around the room dog owners told their pets to sit. Only one or two obeyed.

"Remember, if your dog won't sit, hold his collar

tight with one hand and push his rump down with the other," Ms. Poodlehair said.

Around the room, owners held leashes tight and pushed down on their dogs' rumps. Lance just sat there and watched it all with a bored expression on his face.

Jessica turned to me and spoke in a low voice. "I don't get it. Lance has *never* sat so still in his life."

"Guess he's a quick study," I said.

Next we worked on "stand" and "stay." Half the dogs sat when they should have stood and hardly any of them stayed. But Lance did everything perfectly. Ms. Poodlehair kept giving us funny looks.

"How does he know what to do?" Jessica whispered. "He's never done any of this before."

"It just goes to show you that when he puts his mind to it, he can do almost anything," I whispered back.

Next we practiced "heel." Again Lance performed perfectly, walking beside me around the orange plastic cones, trotting when I jogged, and stopping when I stopped. None of the other dogs "got it."

Ms. Poodlehair seemed less than amused by this. She went over to the wall and picked up a blue hula hoop. "Listen up," she yelled, waving the hoop at everyone. "You've got to spend more time at home working with your dog. You can't just come here once a week and expect that by the end of ten weeks your dog will be jumping through hoops."

Before I could stop him, Lance dashed across the room and jumped through the hoop! Then he quickly turned and jumped back through it in the other direction! Then he stood on his hind legs and hopped around like the trained dogs in the circus!

Ms. Poodlehair put her hands on her hips and glared at Lance, then at Jessica and me.

"Very funny, you two," she fumed. "Bringing a trained animal in here to make the rest of the dogs look like fools. Well, you can get out right now. Hear me! Get out!"

"But — " Jessica started to say.

"I said *leave!*" Ms. Poodlehair yelled.

Jessica and I grabbed Lance and hurried out of the church basement.

"What a snot," I said a few moments later as we walked down the sidewalk toward home.

"Would you mind telling me what's going on?" Jessica asked.

I was tempted to tell her the truth. After all, I never would have gotten out of Mr. Dirksen's body without her help. But Jessica loved Lance more than anything in the world. He was her "poo-chy poo" and her "love puppy." If I told her I'd accidentally switched Lance's body with Andy's, I was afraid she might kill me. I took a deep breath and let it out slowly.

"To tell you the truth, Jessica, I think . . . Lance is just a really smart dog."

15

When we got back to our house, Mom was in the kitchen nuking the dinner Jessica had made.

"So how was obedience school?" she asked.

Jessica and I gave each other sheepish looks.

"Uh, not so good, Mom," Jessica said.

Mom frowned. "Why not?"

"Well, Lance sort of got kicked out," I said.

Mom's jaw dropped. "He was *that* bad?"

"No, he was that *good*," Jessica said.

"I don't understand," said Mom.

Jessica turned to Lance. "Roll over and play dead."

Lance gave her a look that said, "Get real."

"Do it," I said.

Lance let out a big sigh.

Owooooo! He howled and staggered sideways, teetering this way and that, moaning and groaning, and making anguished faces. He banged into the kitchen cabinets, then bounced off the refrigerator, and caromed off the dishwasher. He stumbled over his water bowl, spilling water on the floor, and crashed into the kitchen table. Finally he tumbled onto his back, with his eyes closed, his mouth open, and his tongue hanging out. All four legs pointed toward the ceiling. They twitched a few times. Lance gasped his last breath and went limp.

"See?" Jessica said.

Mom's mouth hung open and her eyes were wide. "How in the world did he learn that?"

"He's a natural actor," I said.

Lance rolled over onto his feet and smiled at us.

"But what about chewing?" Mom asked.

"Are you going to chew anymore?" I asked Lance.

Groof! Lance shook his head.

"Amazing," said my mother.

"Anyone call, Mom?" Jessica asked.

"Josh. He said it was important."

I picked up the phone and dialed Josh's number.

"Hello?" he answered.

"It's me," I said. "What's up?"

"You better get over here," Josh said.

"What's wrong?"

"Everything."

16

Mom wouldn't let me go to Josh's until after dinner. By the time I got there, it was getting dark. I raced up the front walk and rang the doorbell.

"Who is it?" Josh asked from inside.

"Jake."

He pulled open the door and I stepped into his house.

"How's it going?" I asked.

"Don't ask," Josh groaned.

"Where is he?"

"The living room."

I went into the living room and looked around. Besides the couches, chairs, and coffee table, the room looked empty. Then I heard a gnawing sound. It seemed to be coming from under the coffee table. I got down on my hands and knees and looked. Andy was under the coffee table, chewing on a table leg.

Josh came in. "He's been doing that for the last

hour. I think I'm going to have a hard time explaining the table leg to my parents."

"Maybe he's hungry," I said.

"What should we give him?" Josh asked. "Dog food?"

"Naw, let's give him people food. Lance eats just about anything, and so does Andy. It's one of the things they have in common."

"That and not washing," Josh said.

We went into Josh's kitchen and looked in the refrigerator.

"There's some cold chicken," said Josh.

"I don't know," I said. "He might choke on the bones."

"Soup?"

"Better not," I said. "I doubt he'd know how to use a spoon. It could be a real mess."

"Then what?" asked Josh.

"How about something that we eat, that's also like dog food?"

Josh thought for a moment. "I know!" He hurried over to the pantry and took out a can. "Corned beef hash!"

"Perfect!" I said.

Josh started to open the can with a can opener. "Think we should heat it up?"

"Nah, I don't think he'll care," I said. "I'll go get him."

I went into the living room. Andy was still under the coffee table, chewing on the leg.

"Okay, Andy!" I clapped my hands together. "Here you go, boy, come and get it!"

Andy stuck his head out from under the coffee table and looked up at me. His mouth was open and his tongue was hanging out. There were little brown splinters on it.

"Come on, boy, it's time to eat," I said.

Ruff! Ruff! Andy barked at me, but stayed under the coffee table.

"Food. You know, 'Come and get it?' "

I don't know if he understood me, but he crawled out from under the table and followed me into the kitchen on his hands and feet. As soon as he smelled the corned beef hash, he made a beeline for the kitchen table where Josh had put the plate.

We managed to get him into a chair. Ignoring the knife and fork, Andy bent over and pressed his face into the reddish brown corned beef hash.

Josh grimaced. After a few moments Andy paused and looked up at us. His nose, cheeks, and chin were smeared with chunks of hash.

Gruff! he barked.

"I bet he wants something to drink," I said.

"Here." Josh went to the sink and filled a glass.

"No, don't!" I cried.

"Why not?"

"He won't know what to do with a glass. Try a bowl."

Josh poured the water into a bowl and put it on the table next to the plate of corned beef hash.

Andy pressed his face into the water and lapped up some of it. Then he pressed his face back into the hash and ate some more.

"Reminds me of lunchtime at school," I said.

"At least he isn't throwing it," Josh quipped.

It wasn't long before Andy had finished all the hash and water. Wet gooey globs of hash were still stuck to his chin and cheeks.

"Lovely," Josh muttered.

"I can fix it." I went to the sink and ran water on a bunch of paper towels. Then I came back and wiped Andy's face clean.

Ruff! Ruff! Andy barked happily.

"There you go." I dropped the dirty paper towels in the garbage can. "Now, if we're lucky, he'll go to bed and sleep for the rest of the night."

"Uh, I don't think so," Josh said.

"Why not?"

"Look." Josh pointed at Andy, who was still sitting at the table. Only now his legs were pressed tightly together and he had an uncomfortable look on his face.

17

"Uh — oh," I gasped. "You thinking what I'm thinking?"

"It's not like there are a lot of other choices," Josh said.

"Hurry!" I grabbed Andy by the collar and yanked him out of the seat. We ran down the hall to the bathroom. Andy stopped outside and peered in, sniffing apprehensively. I flicked on the bathroom light and pushed him inside, shutting the door behind him.

"Think he'll know what to do?" Josh asked.

"Keep your fingers crossed," I said.

We stood outside the bathroom door and listened. Several minutes passed.

"You hear anything?" I asked.

"Nope. You?"

"*Nada.*"

Then we heard a sound. But it wasn't what we'd expected to hear.

"What's that?" I asked.

Josh pressed his ear to the door. "Sounds like scratching."

"Scratching?" For a second I didn't understand. Then suddenly I did! "He's scratching at the door!"

"Why?"

"Probably because he wants to get out," I said.

"But he didn't do anything," Josh said.

"Yeah, I know." I pulled open the door. Andy was standing there facing us. He still didn't look happy.

"Now what?" Josh asked.

"I don't know," I said.

"Well, I really don't think he should be in the house. Know what I mean?"

"You're right," I said. "We better take him for a walk."

18

We took Andy outside and walked along the sidewalk, under the streetlights. As long as I held him by the collar, he stood upright. Once Andy was outside, he knew what to do. We walked a couple of blocks while he sniffed around. Pretty soon everything was better.

"Phew." Josh looked relieved. "I was really worried there for a moment."

"Hey, he's a smart dog." I patted Andy on the head.

We started back toward Josh's house, walking along the sidewalk in the dark. Except for the way Andy panted and his tongue hung out, he acted almost normal.

"Know what's weird?" Josh said. "We could probably get away with this for a long time. I mean, before anyone noticed that Andy was acting different."

"You think?"

"Sure," Josh said with a grin. "I'm actually starting to like him more this way."

Ruff! Ruff! Suddenly Andy lurched forward and almost got out of my grasp. I held onto his collar and yanked him back. Up ahead a lady was walking toward us with a small white poodle.

Yap! Yap! Yap! the poodle barked back.

Ruff! Ruff! Andy barked.

"My word!" the lady fumed. "Don't you kids have anything better to do than harass people and their pets?"

"Sorry!" Josh slid his arm through Andy's and together we dragged him away.

Ruff! Ruff! Andy kept barking.

"Shut up, you dummy," Josh hissed. "You want to get us in trouble?"

"Let's just get him home," I said, keeping a tight grip on his collar.

But a little farther down the street we turned the corner and came upon a man with a big black dog.

Grrrrr! Ruff! Andy growled and barked again. Josh and I had to tighten our grip on him.

Groof! Groof! the big black dog barked back and strained against his leash.

"What's wrong with you kids?" the man yelled angrily as he held the big black dog back. "Why don't you grow up?"

"Sorry!" I yelled as we quickly pulled Andy away.

"We better get him home before we meet a cat or something," Josh said. We quickened our steps and soon got to Josh's block.

Screeech! Just as we were about to turn up Josh's front walk a police car skidded around the corner with its lights flashing. It stopped in front of Josh's house. The next thing Josh and I knew, we were blinded by a bright spotlight.

"Hold it right there, you three," a deep voice ordered.

19

Josh and I squinted into the light. We could barely see the outline of the police car. I kept a tight grip on Andy's collar. Josh slid a finger through the belt loop in Andy's jeans.

"Come over here," the voice ordered.

Josh and I went back down the walk with Andy. As our eyes adjusted to the bright light, we could see the policeman in the car, shining the spotlight at us. We stopped a few feet away.

"That you, Josh?" the police officer asked.

"Uh, yeah, Officer Parsons," Josh replied.

Since we lived in a pretty small town, we knew some of the cops.

"How's your dad doing?" the policeman asked.

The year before, Mr. Hopka had fallen off a ladder and broken his leg. Officer Parsons must have been one of the cops who answered the call for help.

"He's a lot better, Officer Parsons," Josh said nervously.

"Glad to hear it," said the police officer. "I just got a report of three kids harassing people walking their dogs. That wouldn't be the kind of thing you'd do, would it, Josh?"

Josh swallowed. "Uh, no, sir."

Andy stood between us, panting with his tongue hanging out.

Officer Parsons shined the spotlight on him and frowned. "What's wrong with him?"

"Who?" Josh asked innocently.

"Him." Officer Parsons pointed at Andy. "Why's he breathing like that?"

"Oh, uh, he's been running."

"Why?" asked the cop.

"Wind sprints," I said. "For track."

"At night?" Officer Parsons scowled.

"It was a spur of the moment thing," Josh explained. "When he gets the urge to do wind sprints, there's no stopping him."

Officer Parsons gave Andy a hard look. I wasn't sure he believed us. "You okay, son?"

Ruff! Andy barked back.

"Did he just bark?" Officer Parsons asked.

"Uh, that wasn't a bark, sir."

"Then what was it?" the officer asked.

Josh glanced at me with a pleading look in his eyes.

"Uh, that's how the coach taught him to replenish his oxygen supply," I said. "There's a new theory that barking helps you get your breath back faster. All the runners are doing it."

"Hmm, never heard of that," Officer Parsons said. "Well, they're always coming up with something new, aren't they?"

"Yes, sir, they are," said Josh.

"So you haven't seen those kids, have you?" the police officer asked.

"No, sir." Josh shook his head.

"Okay, Josh, you and your friends better get inside now," Officer Parsons said. "It's getting late."

"Yes, sir," Josh said.

Breathing big sighs of relief, Josh and I turned around and started up the walk. Officer Parsons started to pull away. That's when Andy must have seen something in the dark.

Grrr! Ruff! he growled and barked.

The cop car screeched to a halt.

"Hold it!" Officer Parsons yelled.

20

I felt a cold shiver of fear. Josh and I turned around, keeping Andy in between us. This time I was sure we were dead.

"Get over here," Officer Parsons ordered.

Still holding onto Andy, we stepped back toward the police car.

"Did I just hear him growl and bark?" the police officer asked.

"Uh, no, sir," said Josh.

"That's funny, I could have sworn I heard him growl," said the police officer.

"That's just another part of the breathing exercise," I explained. "You sort of growl in and bark out."

Then to demonstrate, I took a deep breath, making a weird growling sound, and then barked.

Officer Parsons looked at me like I'd completely lost my mind. Just then his police radio crackled on. There'd been an accident a few blocks away, and the police dispatcher asked if he could get over there fast.

"I'll be right there," Officer Parsons said into the mike, then looked back at us. "Go home, boys. I don't want to see you again tonight."

Then he flicked on his flashing lights. *Screech!* He left a small patch of rubber and zoomed away down the street. Andy opened his mouth again to bark, but before he could, Josh and I clamped our hands across his face and stopped him.

Mmmhhmmpphhh! Andy struggled against our grips.

"Get him inside," Josh hissed.

We practically dragged him up the walk and through the front door into the house.

Bang! Josh slammed the door behind us and we let go of Andy. He jumped away and faced us.

Ruff! Ruff! he barked and shook his rear like he thought it was a game.

Josh pressed his fingers into his eyes and shook his head wearily. "Remind me never to get a dog."

"Well, at least we're okay now," I said. The words had hardly left my mouth when we heard a car pull into the driveway and two doors open and slam shut.

Josh's eyes widened. "It's my parents!"

21

Josh looked around in a panic. "We can't let them see him."

"What should we do?" I asked.

"Grab him."

Josh and I got on either side of Andy, who crouched down playfully, looking left and right as if he thought we wanted to play.

"One! Two! Three! Now!" Josh yelled. We both sprang at Andy.

"Unh!" Crash! At the last possible second Andy ducked and slid away. Josh and I crashed into each other and fell in a tangle to the living room floor.

The front door lock clicked. The door swung open and Mr. and Mrs. Hopka started in, wearing their business clothes. Josh and I were sprawled on the floor. His parents stopped and stared at us.

"Josh?" Mr. Hopka scowled.

"Oh, uh, hi, Dad." Josh quickly untangled himself from me and stood up.

Ruff! Ruff! Andy bounded over to the Hopkas, then started to sniff their legs.

"What in the world?" Mrs. Hopka gasped.

"Oh, uh, it's just a joke." Josh lunged for Andy, grabbed him by the collar and yanked him back. "We were, uh, just playing dog tag."

"Dog tag?" Mr. Hopka repeated with a frown.

"Yeah, whoever's it has to act like a dog," Josh said, still holding Andy by the collar. "Now come on, Andy, let's go."

Josh started to drag Andy away toward his bedroom.

Ruff! Ruff! With his tongue hanging out and his rear end wiggling, Andy kept trying to look back at Josh's parents.

"Ha ha! That's funny, Andy!" Josh laughed, pretending it was just a big joke.

Mr. and Mrs. Hopka stood inside the front door with bewildered looks on their faces. Then Mr. Hopka noticed me.

"Jake?" he said. "Isn't it rather late for you to be out?"

"Uh, yeah, in fact, I was just going," I said. "I'll go say good-bye to Josh and Andy."

I turned and hurried down the hall, then pushed open the door to Josh's room and went in. Josh's room was small and super neat. Against one wall was a double bunk bed for sleepovers. Josh was sitting on the lower of the two bunks. Andy was sitting on the floor, panting with his tongue out. His head was tilted sideways and his back leg was bicycling as he tried to scratch his ear.

"I don't know how much more of this I can take," Josh groaned.

"I think your parents want me to leave," I said.

"What about him?" Josh pointed at Andy.

Ruff! Ruff! Andy barked playfully.

"I don't know," I said, rubbing Andy on the head.

"You can't just leave me like this." Josh looked desperate. Unlike Andy and me, he was an only child who'd never had a pet or a younger brother. He wasn't used to this kind of stuff.

Andy rolled over on his back with his arms bent like a dog's.

"Now what?" Josh asked.

"He just wants his tummy scratched," I said, bending over and scratching him.

Josh shook his head wearily. "What am I going to do?"

I rubbed my chin for a second and thought. "Tell me something. Do your parents come in your room much at night?"

Josh shook his head. "Hardly ever. Why?"

Five minutes later we'd strapped Andy into the lower bunk with sheets. Josh had wrapped an Ace bandage around Andy's head so that he couldn't

71

open his mouth. Andy lay on the bunk with his bandaged head on the pillow and a dismayed look on his face. No matter where we went in the room, he followed us with his eyes.

"I hate to say it, but this is really cruel," I said.

"Maybe, but at least I'll get some sleep tonight," said Josh.

"Yeah, and tomorrow we'll — " A thought suddenly struck me. From the expression on Josh's face, I could see that he'd just thought of it, too.

"Tomorrow's school!" we both gasped.

22

I got back to my house a little while later. The lights were on upstairs and off downstairs, which meant everyone was getting ready to go to bed. I let myself in the front door.

"That you, Jake?" my father called from upstairs.

"Yeah, I'll be up in a minute," I called back, then headed to the kitchen to see what Lance was doing. The kitchen was dark, so I reached for a switch and flicked it on.

"*Ah!*" An involuntary cry of surprise burst from my lips. Lance was sitting on a chair at the kitchen table. His forelegs were on the table. He gave me a droll look, as if I were acting like a jerk.

"Hey, don't look at me like that," I said. "I just didn't expect to find you sitting at the table, okay? You're a dog, remember?"

Grrrrrr . . . Lance bared his teeth and let a low growl escape his lips.

"Okay, you're really Andy," I admitted. "But

for now you're a dog and you're supposed to act like a dog. And as far as I know, dogs don't sit at the kitchen table in most houses."

Lance sighed, then got down on the floor. He looked back over his shoulder and gestured for me to follow him around the kitchen counter. On the other side of the counter he stopped and nodded down at his food bowl, then gave me a forlorn look. The bowl was filled with round brown dog pellets. The look he gave me said, "You don't really expect me to eat this stuff, do you?"

"Okay, what do you want?" I went over to the refrigerator and pulled it open.

Groof! Groof! Lance barked.

As usual, the fridge was filled with a mixture of stuff from the supermarket, as well as plastic containers of leftovers. I opened a container.

"Yesterday's spaghetti?"

Lance shook his head, so I tried another container.

"Tuna casserole?"

Lance winced.

"Jell-O?"

Lance lay down on the floor and covered his ears with his paws.

I noticed a package and opened it. Inside was sliced roast beef.

"Roast beef?"

Lance quickly jumped to his feet and wagged his tail. *Arf!*

I put the roast beef on a plate on the floor. Instead of eating it, Lance looked up at me sadly.

"Now what?" I asked.

He trotted over to the kitchen counter and stood up on his hind legs with his paws against the cabinet. *Groof!* he barked at the bread box.

"You want a sandwich?"

Arf!

"Dogs don't eat sandwiches," I said.

Lance gave me another sad look. So I took the roast beef and put it between two slices of bread.

"Happy?" I asked, lowering the plate in front of him.

Groof! Lance went back to the refrigerator and barked at it.

"Let me guess," I said, opening the refrigerator door. "You want a pickle?"

Groof! Lance shook his head.

"Mayo?"

Arf!

So I spread mayonnaise on the sandwich and put the plate back down on the floor.

"Happy now?" I asked.

Arf! Lance bent down and tried to nudge the sandwich with his nose. Then he looked up again at me.

Groof!

"*Now* what?" I asked.

Lance nudged the sandwich with his nose.

"Oh, I get it. You want me to hold the sandwich so you can bite it?"

Arf!

"You're really demanding, know that?" I said. But I picked up the sandwich and held it for Lance, who took a big bite.

"Would you mind telling me what you're doing?"

I looked up and found Jessica in her pink bathrobe standing over me.

23

"Uh . . . I'm giving Lance a sandwich," I said, holding the half-eaten sandwich.

"Really?" Jessica looked at me like I'd lost my mind. "Any particular reason why?"

"Well, I . . . er . . . just thought it might be time for a change," I said. "I mean, imagine being a dog and eating the same dumb dog food every day."

"I never thought about it," my sister said.

"There, you see?"

"The only thing I see is that you're really losing it, Jake."

Lance took another bite of the sandwich and ignored her. I had a feeling it was time to change the subject . . . *fast!*

"So, uh, what're you doing down here anyway?" I asked.

"I'm going to bed." Jessica yawned. "I came down to get Lance."

"Huh?" Then I remembered. Lance slept upstairs almost every night.

"Oh, gee, I think that's a really bad idea tonight," I said.

"Why?" Jessica gave me a puzzled look.

"Well, uh, because, er, Lance has been scratching himself a lot. I'm worried he might have fleas."

"Really?" Jessica looked a little bewildered. "I haven't seen him scratch himself once tonight. And he's been wearing a flea collar for months."

Arf! Arf! Having finished the sandwich, Lance barked up at us happily.

"Well, I wouldn't be surprised if that collar's no good anymore," I said.

"I don't know what's with you, Jake," she said. "I just put a new collar on him a few weeks ago. They're supposed to work for a whole year."

Jessica kneeled down in front of Lance and took his face in her hands. "Jake says you have fleas, poochy poo. He says my little love puppy shouldn't go upstairs tonight."

Grrrrrr! Lance turned to me and growled.

"You don't have fleas, do you, poochy poo?" Jessica kissed him on the head.

Arf! Arf! Lance barked and wagged his tail.

"That's what I thought," Jessica said, straightening up. "Jake's just being a weirdo, like usual. Come on, love pup, let's go."

The next thing I knew, Lance followed my sister out of the kitchen. I swear that he looked back at me with a smile and winked as he left.

24

Lance had a big grin on his face when he followed Jessica into the kitchen the next morning. I gave him a dirty look.

"How'd you sleep?" I asked Jessica.

"Not so well," she said. "Lance kept scratching at my door. I think he wanted to come in."

"You didn't let him, did you?" I asked.

"No way."

I gave Lance an angry look. He gave me a guilty look and slinked away.

"I'm going to talk to you later," I warned him. Then I looked up at the clock and gulped down the rest of my orange juice. "Time to bail."

"But it's too early to go to school," Jessica said.

"I have to stop at Josh's on the way." The night before I'd promised him that I'd help him get Andy to school in the morning.

Jessica gave me a funny look. "You were there until late last night. Now you're going back first thing this morning. What's going on?"

"Why do you think something's going on?"

"Because you're my brother and I know you. It usually takes a national emergency to get you out of bed any earlier than necessary."

"Well, maybe something is going on," I said. "But believe me, you'll be the last to know."

I started out of the kitchen.

Groof! Groof! Lance barked as if he didn't want me to go. I looked down at him still angry that he'd tried to get into my sister's room last night. "What do you want?"

"Another roast beef sandwich, probably," Jessica said.

Arf! Lance barked in agreement.

"Ha!" I had to laugh. "Guess what you can eat, you dirty dog? Dog food."

"Go on, poochy poo." Jessica pointed to Lance's food bowl, which was still full of dog food from the previous night. "Time for breakfast."

Groof? Lance gave me a pleading look. I just smirked. Fat chance, *poochy poo*. This time you can eat it.

A little while later I got to Josh's and rang the bell. "Who is it?"

"The milkman," I said. "Who do you think?"

Josh started to open the door. *Ruff! Ruff!* Andy raced up behind him and through the doorway. Before I could stop him, he threw his arms around my neck and started to lick my face!

"Oh, gross! Get off me!" I pushed him away.

"Guess he's happy to see you." Josh grabbed Andy by the shirt collar and pulled him back into the house.

"Very funny." I wiped my face on my shirt sleeve. I followed them into the house and closed the door behind me. "Look, as soon as school's over today, we have to get Lance and Andy over to Mr. Dirksen's and switch them back."

"Sounds like something happened last night," Josh said.

"Believe it," I replied. "Lance tried to get into Jessica's room last night."

Josh grinned. "Hey, maybe I'll switch bodies with Lance next."

"You do and I'll make sure we get a doghouse."

"I was only kidding," Josh said. "Can't you take a joke?"

"I don't know. Guess my sense of humor is starting to wear a little thin."

"Well, I wouldn't let it wear too thin if I were you," Josh warned.

"Why not?"

Josh pointed at Andy, who was sitting on the floor trying to chew his own shoe. The problem was, it was still on his foot.

"Because now we're going to take this guy to school."

25

The good news was that there was only half a day of school because of teachers' conferences. The bad news was that Andy would have to go. There was no way we could leave him alone at Josh's house, and no way Josh or I could get away with ditching school to keep an eye on him.

Most mornings before school, my friends and I played ball in the yard while we waited for the bell to ring. Sometimes we played soccer, sometimes basketball. That morning they were playing baseball when Josh and I got there.

We were a little late because Andy insisted on stopping to sniff fire hydrants on the way.

"Hey, come on, you guys!" Alex Silver waved when he saw us. "We need some more players!"

Behind Andy's neck, Josh had a tight grip on his shirt collar. "Uh, not today, Alex."

"Come on, guys, don't wimp out!" Alex shouted back. "We need you!"

Ruff! Ruff! Andy barked, clearly eager to join the game. Josh struggled to hold him back.

"Sorry, Alex," I yelled. "No can do."

"You wusses!" Alex shouted. Then he turned around and chucked the baseball high into the air.

Riiiippp!

The next thing I knew, Josh was standing there holding Andy's shirt collar. Only, Andy's shirt wasn't attached to it anymore. Andy, meanwhile, was streaking toward the rolling baseball.

"All right, Andy!" Alex cheered.

Andy grabbed the ball, but instead of throwing it toward the infield, he took off in another direction, away from the field.

"Ever see him run that fast?" Josh asked.

I shook my head. Andy was really moving.

"Hey, come back here!" everyone started yelling. "Give us the ball back, you jerk!"

Andy kept running. Alex turned and yelled at us, "What's with that guy?"

"He's not himself today," I said.

"How come he took the ball?" Alex asked.

"Guess he wanted it," Josh said.

"Well, how about getting it back?"

"You want it?" Josh said. "You can get it."

"Uh, Josh?" I nudged him.

"What?"

"Maybe it would be better if we got it," I said. "Know what I mean?"

Josh and I started to jog after Andy, who had

run all the way to the fence at the edge of school property. There he dropped the ball and then crouched down on the grass behind it, watching us and panting with his tongue out.

"Why do I feel like I've been through this before?" Josh murmured as we walked across the dew-covered grass.

"Maybe it was a mistake to bring him to school," I muttered.

"You expected me to leave him tied up all day on the bunk bed?" Josh asked.

"Why not?"

"Well, for one thing, it's cleaning lady day. For another, I think that's pretty cruel, don't you?"

"I'll tell you when school's over," I said. Andy was still crouched behind the ball, waiting for us.

"What's his problem?" Alex asked as he caught up to us.

"Don't ask," I said.

"Is he going to give the ball back?"

"When he gets like this, you never know."

"What do you mean, when he gets like this?" Alex asked. "Has he gone mental or something?"

As we got closer, Andy rose to his feet and picked up the ball. His eyes darted around as if he was planning his next move.

"We better stop here," I said when we got about thirty feet away.

"Why?" Alex asked. "And why's he panting like that?"

"You'd pant, too, if you'd just run that far."

"Come on, Andy, give the ball back." Alex started toward Andy.

"Don't." I grabbed his arm.

"Why not?" Alex asked.

"As long as he thinks you want it, he won't give it to you."

"What?" Alex looked at me like I was crazy.

"That's just the way he is," I said.

"How am I going to get the ball back?"

"Turn around and walk away like you don't care."

Alex stared at me. "Maybe I was wrong. It's not Andy who's gone mental, it's *you!*"

"Just do it," said Josh.

The three of us turned and started to walk away. Out of the corner of my eye I saw Andy stop panting and frown. Then he stuck his nose in the air and sniffed. Dropping the ball, he started to walk along the fence as if he was following a scent.

"Now's your chance," I whispered to Alex. "Walk slowly toward the ball."

Alex turned and started toward the ball. Meanwhile, Josh and I strolled toward Andy, who watched us warily.

"Now what?" Josh asked out of the corner of his mouth.

I reached into my pocket and took out a couple

of Skittles from a pack I'd bought a few days before. "Hey, Andy, look! Here, boy!"

I held out the candies. Andy squinted, then bounded toward me. The next thing I knew, he bent down and ate them right out of my hand.

Josh winced. "That is totally gross. Why can't he pick stuff up and eat it?"

"Have you ever seen a dog pick up his food and eat it?" I wiped my hand on my jeans.

"He's not a dog," Josh said.

Andy finished the Skittles and bent down again. He stuck his nose next to my pocket and sniffed the rest.

"Tell *him* that," I said.

26

Getting Andy through homeroom wasn't hard. All we had to do was make him stay in his seat. Josh sat on his right and I sat on his left, and we kept our fingers in his belt loops. Every time Andy tried to get up, we just pulled him back down.

"That was easy," I said when we got out into the hall after homeroom and started toward our next class, keeping Andy between us.

"Believe me, it's going to get harder," Josh said.

"At least it's Dirksen's class next," I said. "He's always telling us we act like animals anyway."

We got into the science lab. The second bell hadn't rung yet and everyone was milling around the room. We let go of Andy and he wandered toward the back of the lab, sniffing around the jars of dead bugs and animals in formaldehyde. Josh and I stood a few feet away, just in case he tried to eat something.

"What'd you give him for breakfast?" I asked.

"Popcorn," Josh said.

"What? Why?"

"I tried to think of stuff he could just stick his face into and eat."

Mr. Dirksen came into the classroom and said loudly, "Okay, everyone, take your seats!"

Of course, no one ever listened to him. He usually had to yell at us two or three times before we'd do it.

"I said, 'Sit!' " Mr. Dirksen said even more loudly.

Andy's eyes darted around nervously. Then he sat down on the nearest lab stool.

"Wow, he never did that at home," I said.

"Maybe he's finally learning," said Josh.

But Andy only sat for a second. Then he got up and went back to sniffing the jars.

"I take it back," Josh said.

"This is the last time I'm going to say it, people!" Mr. Dirksen announced crossly. "Either sit or pay a visit to Principal Blanco's office."

Everyone except Andy drifted toward their lab tables and sat on the metal stools. Josh and I both sat down and turned to each other.

"Where is he?" I asked.

"I thought he was with you," Josh said.

We both turned to the back of the room. Andy was back there, sniffing an old human skeleton hanging on a metal hook.

"Hey, Andy, come on!" I hissed.

"Yo, dummy!" Josh whispered.

Andy ignored us.

"Ahem!" Mr. Dirksen cleared his throat. "Andy!"

Andy ignored him, too, and continued to sniff at the skeleton. Now the other kids noticed him.

"What's he doing?" Julia Sacks asked.

"Looks like he's sniffing that skeleton," said Amber Sweeney.

"What does he think he is, a dog?" asked Alex Silver.

Josh glanced at me and whispered, "I'm starting to get a bad feeling about this."

"Andy, this is my final warning," Mr. Dirksen said. "Either sit or go to Principal Blanco's office."

I quickly dug into my pocket and got out a few more Skittles. "Hey, Andy!" I hissed, holding my hand low, where Dirksen couldn't see it.

Andy turned and saw the candies. He quickly joined Josh and me at our lab table. I got him to sit on the stool by holding my hand with the Skittles up high. Then I fed him.

Sitting at the lab table next to us, Julia Sacks looked totally grossed out. "You guys are really sick."

"All right," Mr. Dirksen said. "Today we're going to start a new section on minerals, rocks, and gems. Now, you've probably all seen a diamond on a ring and you know it's very polished and shiny. But what does a diamond look like when it's first found in its natural environment?"

Mr. Dirksen looked around the room for someone to call on. Andy was sitting straight up on his stool with his mouth open and his tongue hanging out.

"Can you tell us, Andy?" Mr. Dirksen asked.

Ruff! Andy barked.

"That's right," said Mr. Dirksen. "Diamonds are rough when first found."

"Good boy." I patted Andy on the head and fed him a few more Skittles.

"Now, of course, what happens to a diamond that transforms it into the glittering gem we see in a jewelry store?" Mr. Dirksen asked.

Ruff! Andy barked.

"Please don't call out, Andy," Mr. Dirksen said.

Ruff! Ruff! Andy barked.

"This is my last warning, Andy."

"Quiet, boy." I quickly pulled more Skittles out of my pocket and fed them to him. This time, Mr. Dirksen saw us.

"May I ask what you're doing, Jake?"

The whole class turned and stared at me. I glanced nervously at Josh, hoping he'd come up with some kind of excuse. But Josh bit his lip and shook his head.

"I'm waiting for an explanation, Jake." Mr. Dirksen crossed his arms.

"Well, er, you see, Mr. Dirksen," I said, "we're doing a project in social studies where we try to look at the world through different eyes. Andy decided to look at it through a dog's eyes."

Mr. Dirksen looked puzzled.

"Lame," Josh whispered out of the corner of his mouth.

"At least I tried," I whispered back.

"Well, he's not buying it."

"Why can't *you* come up with something?" I whispered.

"Hey, it wasn't *my* idea to turn him into a dog," Josh hissed.

"What are you talking about?" I whispered back. *"You're* the one who threw the switch!"

"Yeah? Well *you're* the bonehead who took us to Dorksen's house in the first place!" Josh shot back.

"Big blob o' nothin'," I hissed.

"Pseudopod," Josh hissed back.

"Fungusbrain."

"Sporeface."

"That's enough, you two!" Mr. Dirksen said sternly. "If you have something to say, I suggest you say it to me."

Flap! Just then one of the window shades shot up with a loud noise.

Owwwwooooo! Startled, Andy let out a howl, jumped off his stool, and tore out of the room.

"What the — " Mr. Dirksen gasped.

"I'll go get him!" I yelled and ran out after him.

"Me, too!" yelled Josh and followed.

27

All three of us got sent to Principal Blanco's office. The principal was on the phone, so his white-haired secretary, Mrs. Hub, told us to sit on some wooden chairs outside his door. Andy sat between Josh and me. His tongue hung out and he was really panting hard.

"Nice going, Jake," Josh muttered out of the side of his mouth.

"I'm really getting tired of you blaming me for everything," I snapped.

"No talking, boys," Mrs. Hub warned. "You don't want to get into any *more* trouble, do you?"

Josh and I both shut up. Between us, Andy yawned. Then he put his head on my shoulder and closed his eyes.

"Cut it out!" I whispered and shook my shoulder.

Andy picked up his head, opened his eyes, yawned, then put his head down on Josh's shoulder.

"Bug off!" Josh did the same thing. Andy picked his head up again and put it back on my shoulder. I would have shaken his head off again, but Mrs. Hub tipped her glasses down on her nose and stared at me.

"I hope you two are good friends," she said.

Josh snorted and hid a grin with his hand.

Just then the door to Principal Blanco's office opened and the principal stepped out. Mr. Blanco was a short, pudgy man with curly black hair and narrow eyes. He always wore a black suit and tried to act tough.

"Find something funny, Mr. Hopka?" Recently he'd started to address the students by their last names, as if this somehow made everything more official.

Josh quickly pressed his lips together and shook his head.

Then Principal Blanco looked at me. Andy was still sleeping with his head on my shoulder.

"What's wrong with him?" the principal asked.

"I think he's really tired," I said.

"Why's his shirt torn like that?" Blanco asked.

Jake and I shrugged.

Principal Blanco shook his head in disgust. "I always say you kids don't get enough sleep. What's the point of coming to school if you're too tired to pay attention? All you wind up doing is putting your head down on your desk and going to sleep. That instantly promotes a tone of disrespect toward your teacher, and subtly encourages your fellow students to misbehave. What time do you go to bed at night, Mr. Sherman?"

"Uh, around eleven," I said.

Principal Blanco nodded. "Just as I expected. And what about you, Mr. Hopka?"

"Eleven-thirty," said Josh.

"You see?" Principal Blanco said. "That proves my point. When I was your age I was in bed by nine every night. You kids don't get enough sleep."

"But we're not tired, Mr. Blanco," I said.

Principal Blanco blinked. "Well, you should be. And by the way, when Mr. Kent wakes up, tell him to get a new shirt."

"Will do, sir."

Blanco straightened his tie. "Now, if you'll excuse me, I have an important appointment with the superintendent."

The principal turned to his secretary. "Take phone messages, Mrs. Hub. Tell anyone who calls that I'll get back to them after lunch."

"There's only half a day today," Mrs. Hub reminded him. "Teachers' conferences, remember?"

"Oh, right, in that case tell them I'll call them back tomorrow."

"And what about these boys?" Mrs. Hub pointed at Josh, Andy, and me.

The wrinkles in Principal Blanco's forehead deepened. He turned back to us. "Why are you here, boys?"

"Mr. Dirksen sent us," Josh said.

"Misbehaving in class, huh?" the principal guessed.

"It was his fault." Josh and I simultaneously pointed at Andy, who still had his head on my shoulder with his eyes closed and his mouth open.

Principal Blanco pursed his lips together. "Well, I should probably give him a lecture, but I'm late for my appointment with the superintendent, and anyway, you know what they say about dogs."

Josh and I tensed.

"Let sleeping dogs lie," Principal Blanco said. He turned to his secretary. "I believe it was Winston Churchill who said that. Am I right, Mrs. Hub?"

"Charles Dickens," Mrs. Hub replied tersely.

"Oh, well, what's the difference?" the principal said with a shrug. "Anyway, you boys can sit out the rest of the period here. Then proceed to your third period class. And try to get some sleep tonight, okay?"

"Sure thing, Principal Blanco," Josh and I both said, relieved.

The principal left the office. Andy twitched in

his sleep and stretched his legs and arms straight out from the chair. Mrs. Hub tipped down her glasses and studied him.

"Is he all right?" she asked.

"Just tired," I said.

"*Dog tired*," Josh added.

28

"I can't believe we made it through the whole morning," I said. Josh and I were walking home. Josh was holding Andy by what was left of his shirt collar.

Ruff! Andy stopped next to a fire hydrant and tried to bend down to sniff it, but Josh yanked him back up.

"We may have made it through this morning, but I'm not sure how much more of this I can take," Josh moaned.

"All we have to do is get Lance and Andy over to Mr. Dirksen's garage and switch them back," I said. "Give me about twenty minutes while I go home and get Lance."

"Okay," Josh said. "I'll just stop at my house to dump my books."

I got home and let myself in. I could hear the TV in the den. I went in and found Lance sitting on the couch, watching a talk show.

"Having fun?" I asked.

Lance shrugged and kept watching the TV.

"I guess watching TV doesn't compare with trying to get into my sister's room, huh?" I asked.

Lance shrugged.

"You're a real dog, know that?" I said. "Anyway, it's time to switch you back to your own body. Josh is going to meet us at Mr. Dirksen's."

Lance just stared at the TV and didn't budge.

"Did you hear me? I said we're going to get you back into your body again."

Lance reached down to the remote lying on the couch beside him. He pressed one of the buttons with his paw nail and the volume went up.

"What are you doing?" I asked.

Lance gave me a look that said, "It's obvious, isn't it? I'm watching TV."

"But we've got to get you back into your body," I said.

Lance responded with a yawn. His eyes remained glued to the screen.

I went over and pressed the power button on the TV, turning it off. "Come on, I'm serious."

Click! The TV went back on. Lance did it with the remote.

Click! I turned it off again.

Click! He turned it on again.

"What's with you?" I asked, turning the TV off again.

Click! Lance turned it back on.

"This is ridiculous." I stepped toward the couch and reached for the remote.

Grrrrrrr . . . Lance bared his teeth and growled at me.

I stopped.

Lance turned back to the TV.

I took another step and reached for the remote again.

Grrrrr . . . Lance bared his teeth and growled again.

"I can't believe you," I said. "You actually want to stay in a dog's body?"

The talk show went to commercials. Lance pressed his nail against the remote and turned down the volume. Then he looked at me and nodded.

"But you can't!" I gasped. "You have an obligation to your body. Your parents are coming home tonight. What do you think is going to happen when they figure out that their son has the mind of a one-year-old Labrador retriever?"

Lance shrugged and glanced at the TV as if making sure the talk show hadn't come back on.

"I can't believe this," I groaned. "How can you want to stay in a dog's body?"

Lance gave me a look that said, "Why not?"

I stared at him, reclining there on the couch. Maybe it wasn't so hard to understand. If he stayed a dog, he didn't have to go to school. He could lie around the house all day and watch TV. He could play and sleep and do whatever he wanted.

It wasn't fair . . .

"Forget it!" I snarled. "No way!"

Briiiinnngggg! The phone rang.

"You hear me?" I fumed. "You're not going to get away with this."

The talk show came back on. Lance pressed the remote and the volume went back up.

Briiiiinnnnngggg!

I almost told Lance not to go anywhere, but it didn't seem necessary. I went into the kitchen and answered the phone.

"Jake? It's Josh."

"Hi," I said. "I guess you're wondering why I'm not at Mr. Dirksen's. Well, I'm having a problem with Lance. He doesn't want to go."

"Neither does Andy."

"Why won't Andy go?" I asked.

"Well, we got back to my house and he saw a squirrel."

"So? He's seen squirrels before."

"I know, but he's never chased one up a tree before," Josh said.

"Sure he has. He always chases them up trees."

"But he doesn't usually follow them."

"*What!?* Dogs don't climb trees," I said.

"Maybe not, but dogs in human bodies do," said Josh. "Anyway, once he got up the tree he must've remembered that he was a dog. So now he's freaked because he can't figure out how to get back down."

"Can't you help him?"

"I tried, but he won't let go of the branch he's on," Josh said. "Anyway, what's up with Lance?"

"He doesn't want to go back into his old body."

"Why not?"

"Because this way he doesn't have to go to school. He can just lie around all day and watch TV and sleep."

"I don't blame him."

"Neither do I, but I'd rather have my dog back."

"So what are you going to do?" Josh asked.

"I don't know," I said. "Guess I'll have to think of something. Meanwhile, I'll come over and help you get Andy out of the tree."

"Take your time," Josh said.

"Why?"

"Because if we're not going to switch them I'd just as soon leave him there for a while. Believe me, I could use a break."

29

I went back to the den. Lance was still watching TV.

"Let me ask you something," I said. "What do you think is going to happen when Jessica and my parents come home? You think they won't notice that you're sitting on the couch with the remote?"

Lance ignored me.

"What are you going to do when my mother tells you to get off the couch?" I asked. "You going to bare your teeth and growl at her? You know what she'll do? She'll take you to the pound and leave you there for good."

Lance gave me a look like I was being an idiot.

"Oh, I get it," I said. "You've already thought of all this stuff. You figure all you have to do is act like a dog when they're around and everything will be cool, right? And as soon as they leave for school and work you'll be back on the couch watching the tube."

Without taking his eyes off the TV, Lance smiled and nodded.

"Well, I'll tell you one thing, dude, you can forget about me giving you anything good to eat," I said. "You want to be a dog? Fine, you can eat dog food."

Lance just shrugged. Apparently he'd already thought about that, too, and was willing to accept it.

I tried every argument I could think of. I reminded him that a dog lives roughly seven years for each human year and that by the time I was in my twenties he'd be a rickety old mutt. I reminded him that he'd never get his driver's license or be able to vote. I talked about all the parties and ball games he'd miss. But nothing I said made a dent.

Andy had decided to spend the rest of his life as a dog.

After a while, we heard the front door click. Lance quickly turned off the TV and got down off the couch. He trotted toward the door, reaching it just as Jessica let herself in.

"Oh, look who's here! It's my little love puppy!"

Groof! Groof! Lance barked happily.

Jessica rubbed his head affectionately. "My little poochy poo missed me! How sweet!"

Meanwhile, Lance turned to me and grinned as if he was saying "See? I know how to act like a dog when I have to."

"Mom and Dad are coming home late tonight," Jessica said when she saw me. "Mom said I should make some frozen pizzas for dinner."

It didn't take long for her to heat up the pizzas. Just before we sat down to eat, Jessica filled Lance's bowl with dog food. Lance seemed pretty reluctant to eat it. I watched as he sniffed it and sort of grimaced. Then he looked over his shoulder at me with a pleading look, as if to say, "Please help me out of this!"

I shook my head and gave him a look that said, "No way, dude. You want to live like a dog, you're going to eat like one, too."

Lance narrowed his eyes and silently bared his teeth at me. Then in defiance, he plunged his snout into the dog food and started to eat. He gobbled it all down pretty quickly, the same way I used to eat broccoli — like he wanted to get it over with fast.

When the bowl was empty he looked up at me again. I pointed a finger into my mouth like I wanted to make myself barf.

"What are you doing?" Jessica asked.

"Huh?" I quickly spun around in my seat. "Oh, uh, nothing."

Across the kitchen, Lance gave me a smug smile.

"Oh, poochy poo, come here." Jessica held out her arms toward Lance, who trotted over. My sister gave him a big hug and rubbed him on his head.

"You are the best dog in the world, know that?" Jessica bent her head down and Lance licked her face and ears. "That's right, my big poochy poo love puppy."

If only she knew, I thought with a groan.

Lance opened his mouth and panted. He grinned at me like he knew what I was thinking. I could see that he loved taunting me. Jessica hugged him again.

"Yes, this is my big big boy, my poochy poo," she said in that dumb lovey dovey voice. "And you know what I did today, my big brave love pup?"

Groof! Lance barked happily. Man, what a life. Never going to school. Watching TV all the time. Having my sister slobber all over him. Maybe he was right. Maybe it was better to be a dog.

"Today," my sister continued, "I made an appointment for you to go to Groomingdales."

The furrows in Lance's forehead deepened slightly. He glanced questioningly at me.

"That's the dog grooming place in town," I said.

Lance turned to Jessica and gave her an apprehensive look.

"You see, Lance, my little love pup," my sister said. "You're getting to be a big grown-up boy now and I've noticed that you smell a little cheesy. And sometimes you scratch people by accident. Now, don't get upset, it's perfectly natural" — Jessica paused and pretended to sniff as if the thought of Lance smelling saddened her — "but we can't have Dad complaining about how you smell. Or that your nails are too long . . . so guess what?"

Lance's eyes grew wide with terror.

"We're going to have you washed, clipped, and perfumed," Jessica said.

30

I thought Lance's eyes were going to bulge right out of his head. *Washed and perfumed?* he must have been thinking. Does she mean, *bathed and smelling like a girl!?*

Owoooo! Lance let out a howl. The next thing I knew, he clamped his teeth around the cuff of my pants and started to pull as hard as he could.

"What's with him?" Jessica asked.

"I, uh, think he must really want to go for a walk," I said, getting up.

Arf! Arf! Lance let go of my leg and barked eagerly. I got his leash.

"Since when do you like taking him for walks?" Jessica asked skeptically.

"Hey, why not?" I said. "Maybe I'll take him for a long walk. It's a nice evening."

"What are you talking about? It's raining."

I looked out the kitchen window. She was right. The sky was gray and rain was splattering against the glass.

"Well, I still feel like taking a walk," I said.

Jessica gave me a strange look. "Be my guest."

I went down to the front closet and got out a jacket with a hood. Then I clipped the leash to Lance's collar and we went out.

"Guess you had a change of heart, huh?" I said as we quickly walked through the rain toward Josh's house.

Lance didn't answer or even look at me. He just pulled as hard as he could on the leash, as if he couldn't wait to get to Mr. Dirksen's and switch back into Andy's body.

"Nah, maybe you're right," I said, slowing down. "Maybe you should stay in Lance's body."

Lance turned around, bared his teeth at me, and growled.

"Oh, yeah, Mr. Tough Guy," I taunted him. "I'm starting to think your bark is worse than your bite."

Before I had time to react, Lance clamped his sharp teeth around my ankle. He squeezed just hard enough to let me know he was serious. Then he let go.

"On the other hand," I said as we started to walk again. "I'd sort of like to get the old Andy back, too."

31

We got to Josh's house and I rang the doorbell. Josh pulled open the door and looked surprised.

"Jake, what are you doing here?"

"Lance had a sudden change of heart," I said. "He wants to be Andy again."

Josh looked down at Lance. "What happened? I thought you liked being a dog."

Groof! Lance barked.

"I think he liked it until Jessica decided it was time to have him groomed," I said.

Josh grinned.

"So where's Andy?" I asked.

"Oh, uh, out back."

"You mean outside?" I said. "It's raining."

"Dogs stay outside," Josh said sheepishly.

"He's not a dog, he's Andy Kent, your friend," I said, and started across the wet grass toward the back of the house.

Josh grabbed a jacket and caught up to me.

"Maybe he is my friend, but it's a real pain to keep him in the house, okay? He chews on all the furniture, he makes a mess when he eats, and he's always going in and out anyway."

Andy was sitting about twelve feet up in a tree in Josh's backyard. His clothes were soaked, his hair was plastered down on his head, and rain water was running down his face. He was hugging himself and shivering. His teeth were even chattering. I turned to Josh.

"I can't believe you left him out here. What were you going to do, leave him out all night?"

"At least I knew he wouldn't go anywhere," Josh said with a shrug.

Ruff! Ruff! Andy barked plaintively at me. He must've been freezing to death!

"Let's get a ladder and bring him down," I said.

Josh went back to the house. I could imagine how Andy wound up in the tree. He must have been so excited about chasing the squirrel that he'd scrambled right up the branches without thinking. But once he'd gotten up there, he'd had no idea how to get down.

Josh came back with a long aluminum extension ladder. We placed it against the tree so that it reached Andy.

"Okay, Andy," I yelled. "All you have to do is climb down this ladder."

Andy stayed huddled in the branches above, probably shivering as much from fear as from the

111

cold. It occurred to me that he had no idea what a ladder was.

"Come on," I urged him.

He wouldn't budge.

"You have to come down," I said.

Andy just whimpered.

"Guess I have to go up and get him," I said and started up the ladder. When I got to Andy, I reached up and tried to grab his ankle. He yanked it away.

"You can't stay here," I said. "If you come down, you can switch bodies with Lance."

Groof! Below me, Lance barked.

Ruff! Andy barked back at him, but still wouldn't budge.

I looked back down at Josh. "Any ideas?"

"We could cut the tree down," Josh said.

"With Andy in it?" I raised an eyebrow. "He could be killed."

Josh shrugged. "It was just an idea."

Groof! Groof! Lance barked excitedly.

"What's he saying?" Josh asked.

"How would I know?" I asked.

Ruff! Andy barked back at Lance.

Groof! Groof! Groof! Lance barked excitedly and wagged his tail.

Arf? Andy barked.

Groof! Lance barked.

Arf! Andy stuck his foot toward me.

"Wow! I think he wants you to help him come

112

down," Josh said. "Lance must've talked him into it."

I guided Andy's foot to a lower branch, and then his other foot to the top of the ladder.

Ruff! Ruff! Andy barked nervously.

"That's a boy, you're doing fine," I reassured him.

Ruff! Ruff! Andy barked uncertainly and came down slowly. Soon he had both feet on the ladder, then both hands. Josh reached up and helped him put one foot below the other while I held him steady.

Finally he reached the ground.

Groof! Groof! Lance barked at him. Andy turned to me.

Ruff! He barked and pawed at my pocket with his hand. Suddenly I realized why he'd come down from the tree.

"You told him I'd give him Skittles?" I said to Lance.

Arf! Lance barked and nodded.

"Hey, smart dog," Josh said.

"He's Andy, not a dog," I said.

Ruff! Andy swiped at my pocket again.

"Hey, sorry, bud, but I ran out," I said.

Ruff? Andy looked surprised and disappointed.

Groof! Groof! Lance barked angrily at me as if he was ticked off that I hadn't brought any Skittles.

"If you're so smart, how come *you* didn't bring any?" I asked.

Groof! Groof! Lance barked.

"I don't care if you're a dog," I said. "You could have taken some money and gone to the store."

Groof! Groof! Lance barked and shook his head.

"That's not true!" I argued. "They'd sell Skittles to an amoeba if he had the money."

"Amoebas aren't really male or female," Josh reminded me. "They're just its. Remember we learned that in school?"

"Thank you for that enlightening information," I grumbled. "Meanwhile, Andy's parents are going to be home in an hour, and they're going to find out that while their son stayed at your house he learned to chew on shoes and chase squirrels. Somehow I don't think they're going to be real thrilled."

"Hey, I'm not the one who insisted on showing everyone that dumb experiment," Josh yelled.

I was tempted to yell back at him, but I caught myself. "Don't you ever get tired of blaming everyone? I mean, it doesn't matter who's right or wrong. The only thing that matters is fixing it before it gets worse."

"Yeah, well, it's *still* not my fault!" Josh insisted.

He just didn't get it.

Groof! Groof! Groof! Lance stepped between us and barked.

"What'd he say?" Josh asked.

"I'm not sure, but it was probably something like 'Shut up and stop arguing because what's going to happen to us is nothing compared to what's going to happen to *him* if we don't get him switched.' "

Arf! Lance nodded emphatically.

32

We started toward Mr. Dirksen's house with Andy and Lance.

"What if Dorksen's home?" Josh asked as we walked down the street.

"We'll just have to tell him what happened," I said. "Given the choice, I'd rather face him than Andy's parents."

"Good point," Josh agreed.

But Mr. Dirksen wasn't there. It had started raining harder and we could hear the distant crash of thunder and see the flicker of far-off lightning.

"Come on." I pulled open the garage door and let everyone in. Then I pulled it down and turned on the light inside.

"Now what?" Josh asked.

I pointed at one of the cages. "Lance, get in that cage."

Arf! Lance did as he was told.

"What about Andy?" Josh asked.

Andy was on the other side of the garage, sniffing Mr. Dirksen's garbage cans.

Outside, a bolt of lightning lit up the sky.

Boom! Thunder crashed. The lightbulb in the garage flickered.

"Storm's coming closer," Josh said nervously.

"Get Andy," I said. "Put him near the cage. When I count to three, push him toward the cage and jump back."

"This better work," Josh muttered as he went to get Andy.

"Hey," I said. "It can't get any worse."

Lance waited in his cage. Josh brought Andy over to the other cage. Andy's tongue was hanging out and he was panting.

"You know, it's too bad we have to switch them," Josh said. "I'm kind of getting used to Andy like this. I may even like him better this way."

"Forget it," I said. "His parents'll kill you. Okay, one and two and three, now!"

Josh gave Andy a shove toward the cage and I pulled down the big red switch. *Ka-boom!* Just at that moment a huge flash of lightning lit up the garage and a giant clap of thunder crashed above. The garage went dark and filled with vapor and heavy fog. For a moment I couldn't see anything.

"Jake, you okay?" Josh called through the mist.

"Yeah, you?"

"Yeah."

Groof!

"Who was that?" Josh asked.

"Andy?" I said.

"Huh?"

"Andy, that you?" I stretched out my arms and tried to feel my way through the thick dark mist.

"Huh?"

The light went back on and the vapor started to disappear. Through the mist I could see Andy . . . only he didn't look exactly like Andy. His face sort of came to a point and the end of his nose was black. His hands looked like a dog's paws without the fur.

"Oh, no!" Josh gasped.

I spun around and looked at Lance, whose dog face was squashed flat. His paws were huge and sort of resembled furry human hands and feet.

Josh and I gaped at each other in amazement.

"Andy?" I said.

"Huh?" He seemed really out of it.

I turned to Lance. "Here, Lance!"

"Huh?" Lance seemed pretty out of it, too.

"What's with them?" Josh asked.

"I'm not sure," I said, "but I have a funny feeling they're both like, half-human, half-dog."

"Oh, great!" Josh groaned. "And I thought you said it couldn't get worse."

33

"Something must have happened to the electricity because of the storm," I said.

"So what do we do now?" Josh asked.

"Try again, I guess."

"Wait a minute." Josh hesitated. "What if it gets even worse? I mean, what if Andy gets Lance's tail next? Or Lance gets Andy's head? We're supposed to be switching their minds, not their body parts."

"You want to leave them like this?" I asked.

Lance was staring down at one of his large hand-shaped paws with a perplexed look on his squashed face. Andy was trying to scratch his left ear with one of his paw-hands.

"You're right," Josh said. "Let's get 'em back to the cages."

We put Lance and Andy in the cages again. Outside the thunder was still crashing.

"Here goes nothing!" I pulled down the switch.

Whomp! This time there was a huge flash and a killer jolt.

Once again the room filled with mist.

"Josh?" I said.

"I'm here," Josh replied. "Andy?"

"Huh?"

"Not again," Josh groaned.

"Not what again?" a voice asked.

"That you, Josh?" I said.

"No, I thought it was you," said Josh.

"It was me," the voice said.

"Who?" I asked.

"Andy."

Groof!

"Who said *that*?" Josh asked.

Groof!

"Sounds like Lance," I said.

"Hey, guys, I think you did it," Andy said. "I'm back."

The fog in the garage began to clear.

Andy was standing near his cage. "Wow, guys, can you believe it? I was Lance!"

Josh and I nodded, dumbfounded.

"I mean, what a trip," Andy was saying. "To tell you the truth, it wasn't so bad. I mean, dog food's a lot better than you might think."

Josh and I nodded, still speechless.

Andy frowned. "What's with you guys? Everything's turned out fine. How come you're not talking?"

Josh and I glanced nervously at each other.

"You want to tell him?" Josh asked.

"No, you tell him," I said.

"What are you talking about?" Andy asked.

"You tell him, Jake," Josh said. "None of this would have happened if it wasn't for you."

"What difference does it make now?" I asked.

"I'm just saying, if anyone tells him, it should be you," Josh said.

"That's the dumbest logic I've ever heard," I said. "It makes absolutely no sense."

"*Guys!*" Andy shouted. "What do you have to tell me?"

"Go on." Josh pointed at me.

I turned to Andy. "Well, uh, it's not really a big deal . . ."

"You could always have plastic surgery," Josh suggested.

Andy started to look pale. "Why? What's wrong?"

"Well, uh, it's your ears," I said.

"My ears?" Andy felt his ears. They were long, and pointed, and covered with short yellow fur. And they hung down to his chin.

34

"**O**h, no!" Andy gasped.

Groof! barked Lance.

We all turned and looked at him. He looked mostly like Lance, except for his ears, which were small, pink, and human-shaped.

"You have to do something!" Andy insisted desperately.

"I don't know, Andy," Josh said, rubbing his chin. "It's sort of an interesting look."

"They could always use you on *Star Trek*," I said.

"This isn't funny, guys!" Andy gasped.

"Actually, it is pretty humorous," Josh said.

"Think of how many earrings you could hang on those things," I said.

"Yuk, yuk," Andy laughed sourly. "You guys are a real scream. Now how about it?"

It took a few moments to get Lance back to his cage. He was pretty much a dog again, and just wanted to play. Fortunately the garage door was down and he couldn't run away.

"Ready!" I yelled when I'd gotten him into the cage.

Josh pulled on the switch.

Whomp! Another lethal jolt filled the garage with mist.

When it cleared, Andy was standing there, feeling his ears. "How do they look?" he asked anxiously.

"They're okay," I said. Andy had his old ears back.

"You swear?"

"I swear."

Groof! Groof! Lance scratched at the garage door and wagged his tail. He wanted to go out.

"Looks like it stopped raining," Josh said.

I checked my watch. "Yeah, and Andy's parents are going to be at your house any minute."

35

We headed back to Josh's house.

"Wow, guys, I still can't believe I was a dog," Andy was saying.

"Well, the important thing is that you're okay and back to normal," I said, slapping him on the back. "You are back to normal, right?"

Ruff! Andy barked.

Josh and I froze and gave each other horrified looks.

"Hey, come on." Andy grinned. "It was just a joke."

Josh and I relaxed.

"Whew, you really had us going there for a second," I said, breathing a sigh of relief.

"You guys . . ." Andy smiled. But then he stopped and stuck his nose up in the air.

"What is it?" Josh asked.

"Don't you smell it?" Andy said, quickly looking around.

"Smell what?"

"A squirrel!" Andy raced across the street and chased a squirrel up a tree. He pressed his hands against the tree trunk and stared up.

Josh and I laughed.

"Very funny!" Josh yelled.

"Yeah!" I joined in. "You're a regular comedian!"

But Andy didn't move from the tree. Then I noticed that Lance was sitting at the end of the leash and didn't seem to smell anything. And he hadn't stopped to sniff any hydrants on the way home either.

"Okay, Andy," Josh yelled. "We got the joke. Come on, dude, we better get back to my house before your parents get there."

Andy came back toward us and we started walking to Josh's house again.

"Wow, I can't believe you guys couldn't smell that squirrel," Andy said.

"Believe me, Andy," Josh said. "We got the joke the first time."

"It was no joke, guys," Andy insisted.

"Who cares anyway?" Josh asked. "It was just a squirrel."

Andy made a face like Josh couldn't be serious. Josh and I traded a furtive glance.

"You *sure* he's back to normal?" Josh whispered.

Just then we heard the far-off bark of a dog a few blocks away. Andy stopped and I could have sworn his ears perked up. At that same moment, Lance just yawned and didn't seem to care at all.

I wouldn't have thought much about it, except that when Lance yawned, he held his paw up to his mouth.

You really had to wonder. . . .

About the Author

Todd Strasser has written many award-winning novels for young and teenage readers. Among his best known are *Help! I'm Trapped in the First Day of School*, *Help! I'm Trapped in My Teacher's Body*, and *Please Don't Be Mine, Julie Valentine!* His next project for Scholastic will be a series about a dog detective named Furry Mason.

Mr. Strasser speaks frequently at schools about the craft of writing and conducts writing workshops for young people. He lives in a suburb of New York with his wife and children.